THE SOUND OF THE LIGHT

by Harriet R. Thorne

To
Angie,
Enjoy!
- J.L. Ford

This book is a work of fiction. Names, characters, places, and incidents either are products of the author's imagination or are used fictitiously. Any resemblance to actual persons, living or dead, events, or locales is entirely coincidental. Despite the fact that you can search the Internet and hear the musical pieces mentioned, and find some of the places used, everything in this book is fiction - descriptions, people, activities, and history.

Visit Mrs. Ford's website at www.Cattail.Nu .

Printed in the United States of America

First Published: September 2020

Cattail.Nu

v.3

Print version:

ISBN-13:

ISBN-10:

Chapter 1

On her seventeenth birthday, her Highness, Princess Sophie Renault of the Laparian Kingdom, was to receive a new slave as a gift from her brother, Wyatt. Sophie dreaded the upcoming evening. No gift from Wyatt was ever really a gift and his presents got more horrific every year...

Sophie controlled her breathing, forcing her body to soft stillness. The danger was real. Wyatt's eyes sparkled and his tongue licked his lips. He was practically bouncing on his toes. Sophie wondered if Wyatt's video surveillance of the room was already set to go directly to his suite in their castle.

"Do you see one you like, dear sister?" Wyatt's voice echoed in the bare cement room.

The selection of potential slaves were lined up in front of them, heads meekly bowed. The bright spotlights that illuminated them had to be hot. Their skin glistened with perspiration. The only slave with any merit, using her brother's standards, looked like a recently conscripted guard. The way the man's pupils contracted when her brother approached him confirmed it; the man had spent time with Wyatt.

This slave would report back to Wyatt and would do as he said, not as Sophie requested. Wyatt was definitely planning on inserting his own creature into her staff. Had Sophie shown too much concern for Pieran and Blair, her current house slaves, or did Wyatt still think of them as things to be used for amusement? If she had, he would kill them.

"This one looks sturdy enough," Wyatt said, reaching out to stroke the man's cheek.

"We could walk faster if you'd stop shoving us!" a man's deep growl echoed from the hallway.

"Shut up, slave!" came the response.

"We're free men, not slaves," another male voice said.

"You'll be dead men if you don't shut up."

Wyatt glanced in the direction of the voices. He put his forefinger in his mouth and sucked it briefly, before pulling it free with a loud kissing pop. "Fresh meat?" He strode off toward the sound.

Pieran, silent at Sophie's side, stepped out of her way as she rushed after Wyatt. Sophie glanced back and saw that he did not follow.

In the hallway, Sophie's brother had already stopped the guards leading two men. The chained men were dressed as simple town folk in rough brown workmen pants with thick, cotton shirts. Their proud bearing suggested otherwise. More guards posing as slaves to infiltrate her suite? They were both handsome, but the taller of the two more so.

Sophie peered at Wyatt. He was flushed and his eyes were wide with arousal. If she didn't do something, both men would be in one of Wyatt's dungeons before the hour was up. Sophie pointed at the shorter of the two men. "I want that one."

One of the guards leading the two men tilted his head respectfully and said, "I'm sorry, Your Highness. These two aren't trained yet."

Wyatt stepped up to the guard. "Did you just deny my sister?" His words dripped with threat.

"No, Your Highness," the guard said quickly, backing up a step. He bowed low. "Of course she can have him. I'll have him cleaned and brought to her suite immediately."

The taller of the two chained men spat. "No! We aren't slaves!"

Sophie panicked. Her brother was about to order them both to his dungeon for training. She could see it in his posture, the way his heels were rising as he rocked onto the balls of his feet. "You're right, of course," she said to the guard. "They both need training. Take mine, give him 30 lashes, and then bring him to me. His friend is going to need more work. Take him to the furnace pit. 5 lashes, every hour, for the next two days."

"No, I want that one," Wyatt said, pointing at the taller man.

Sophie linked her arm into her brother's arm and leaned into him and purred, "Would you deny me this pleasure on my birthday, Your Highness? Surely, you can wait two days." She never called him by his given name; Wyatt liked the power of his title.

Wyatt studied her and reached out and pushed some of her hair behind her ear. His eyes promised retribution. "Very well, dear sister." He turned to the guard, "Why are you still here? You heard my sister. Lead the way. We'll come watch."

The taller of the two fought when the guards tried to separate him from his friend, but he was overwhelmed, beaten, and dragged away.

Sophie pretended to enjoy the whipping, under Wyatt's calculating gaze. She even ordered another 10 strokes when it didn't look like 30 would be sufficient for her purpose. She needed the man too damaged to participate in whatever it was Wyatt had planned that night.

When the guards finished and took the man to be cleaned, Wyatt followed to supervise that too. Sophie excused herself to go prepare for Wyatt's arrival and to make certain that dinner would be ready. She hurried back to collect Pieran.

As soon as they were out of the slave area, she whispered to Pieran, "Furnace pit. New arrival. Get him out."

"It's too soon to use the network again," Pieran replied in an equally hushed tone. "It's too dangerous."

"Go do it right now or he'll be in a dungeon as soon as my brother gets done admiring my new slave. Please," she begged.

Pieran swore under his breath and jogged off.

Back at her suite, Sophie found Blair in the kitchen. The old woman had multiple pots heating on the stove's burners.

"Well?" Blair asked, basting the chicken in the oven. "Are we getting a spy?"

"It's going to be a bad night, Blair."

"Your birthday is always a bad night."

"It's going to be worse. I'm not sure I can do it."

"What happened?"

"I just ordered a man whipped," Sophie confessed.

"Oh?" Blair's voice stayed steady, not curious, but avidly listening.

"My new slave. If I hadn't selected him, Wyatt would have taken him to a dungeon. He's handsome, Blair. Really handsome, and he's proud. Wyatt is going to destroy him if he's not already an agent."

"I'll mix up something to keep him docile." Blair sighed. "You just redirect what you can to me and Pieran. We already know what to expect. Where is Pieran?"

"Hopefully getting my new slave's friend out."

"Lucky one."

"Only if Pieran can get to him before Wyatt."

"Start the gravy, Your Highness. I'll dig out the med kit."

Sophie nodded.

****

A drab grey lizard ran across the balcony railing. It paused and tilted its head toward the afternoon sun. As if on cue, a cloud moved in front of the sun, throwing a foreboding shadow across the rock garden below and the balcony. The lizard slipped down the post and disappeared between the deck slats.

Blair sighed and stretched. She needed to get back to work preparing dinner for Sophie and the Prince. The suite was already as clean as she and Pieran could make it. She'd even polished the claws on the feet of the antique sofa. She'd done everything she could to avoid repercussions. If the Prince killed her that night, it wouldn't be her fault. He might anyway, but it wouldn't be her fault.

Even the rock garden had been checked. She and Pieran had walked it barefoot that morning, making sure the stones were secure in the soil, with no sharp points facing upwards. Blair took one last look at the rock garden below and went back inside, wiping a tiny speck of dust off of the glass door as she passed by.

Every light in the suite was on. That was a subtle thing, begging whatever gods existed to keep the darkness away. It never worked, but they did it every year anyway. This year had potential to be devastating. She hoped Sophie was getting some rest, but most likely, she was just lying in bed staring at her ceiling.

The oven buzzer sounded and Blair hurried to turn it off and check the bird again. She leaned to the side to avoid the blast of oven heat when she opened the door. Did it have enough basil and garlic to complement but not overpower the rosemary? It smelled delicious, but it had to be perfect. Anything could set the Prince off on a violent rampage. If only they had a guaranteed way to kill him. They didn't have the resources. Besides, they needed to kill the King at the same time or it would become impossible and the torturing of innocents would go on. It couldn't be poison anyway. Both the King and Prince always used food tasters.

She transferred the cheesecake from the freezer to the refrigerator so it would be the right balance of cold to creaminess. Then she wiped the pristine surfaces again.

Blair prayed constantly for an end to this misery. The Prince would eventually find a way to kill the King and he would take Sophie into one of his dungeons. The Prince had promised that eventuality. Both Blair and Pieran would be dead or they'd wish they were. The annual birthday party was merely the Prince's idea of a reminder and his appetizer. He couldn't physically torture Sophie yet so he focused on mentally torturing her. The damage he did to Blair and Pieran was merely designed to upset Sophie. Every year, Blair prayed to survive the night. Until during the night, when she prayed not to.

Blair heard the suite's front door open and heard Sophie direct the guards to hang her new slave by the wrists on the platform designed for the purpose. The platform and its rigging had been a present from the Prince eight years prior and it had seen use every year thereafter. Blair had been displayed on it herself several times.

Blair waited until she heard the guards leave and took the prepared drink out into the large sitting room.

Sophie was sitting as still as an ice sculpture on the sofa facing the platform. Blair saw she'd chosen a soft blue gown with a deep V neckline that showed off her new curves. It might be enough to distract the Prince. Blair glanced over at the man on the platform. No low cut dress was going to distract from that. No wonder Sophie was panicked.

Blair went over to Sophie. "A drink, Your Highness?"

Sophie waved her hand and said caustically, "Give it to him. I don't want it."

"Certainly, Your Highness." Blair curtseyed and went over to the man. His hair was still damp from being washed, and the fresh welts had been sealed with a sticky substance. He looked angry, not beaten. He was magnificent. With his chiseled muscles and godlike features, he radiated power. If he were still alive and sane in the morning, it would be a miracle.

"Here, drink," Blair said, holding the cup to the man's mouth.

"I don't want it," he snarled, glaring in Sophie's direction.

Blair took several deep breaths and tried not to fall into hopeless despair. Desperately, she tried asking for sympathy. She leaned close to him. "Please drink it," she breathed. "You'll get me in trouble." How much of a lie was it? Until they knew if this man could be trusted, Sophie had to pretend that she was like the Prince, and if that meant more than just sharp words, it had to be.

The man frowned, but drank.

Blair only let him have half of it. She hoped she had the dosage right. It was hard to judge. His weight and muscles would make him more resistant to the drugs, but the recent whipping would render him more susceptible. She had added a painkiller along with the opiates. If he survived, maybe they could find a way to get him out.

Pieran arrived and bowed to Sophie. "I'm sorry for taking so long, Your Highness."

"I don't want to hear your excuses. Go help in the kitchen."

"Yes, Your Highness." With a subservient bow, he did as instructed and Blair followed him.

"Did you get that man's friend out?" Blair asked, keeping her voice low.

Blair could barely hear Pieran's reply. "Yeah, but there'll be serious repercussions in the morning. It was a mistake. We can't save individuals. We have to save the kingdom."

"It's her birthday. She's not thinking clearly." Blair put her hand on his arm, feeling the heat there.

"Are any of us? It's going to be a bad night. I apologize for anything I'm forced to do to you tonight."

Blair pulled him closer and brushed her lips on Pieran's. "Same, my love."

****

Pieran hurt, but it was tolerable. He could still stand and move. He watched until the Prince was gone across the castle's main courtyard and then he limped back to the suite. Ignoring Sophie, who was still sitting on the sofa, as well as the man on the platform, Pieran went first to Blair and carefully picked her up and carried her soft, shaking body back to her bedroom. He set her on the bed, adjusted the pillow, and pulled the sheet over her. She moaned. The doctor was waiting for their call so she wouldn't be in pain long. He kissed her forehead and promised to return soon.

He went back out to the sitting room. Sophie was standing near the sofa. Her eyes were vacant, but she managed a suitably harsh command, as if her slaves had suddenly annoyed her. "Get the guards in the hallway to help you carry him to his room. You won't be able to lift him by yourself."

Pieran gave her a partial bow. The Prince definitely had plans for the semi-conscious man dangling from his wrists. "Of course, Your Highness." Pieran went to the door and got the guards. With some difficulty, they were able to maneuver the man to a bed. They lay him face down and Pieran made him as comfortable as possible. The man's gaze suggested he was coherent and screaming underneath his drugged inability to move.

Back in the sitting room, Pieran dismissed the guards, who were the Prince's men, and as soon as they were gone, he turned to Sophie and said quietly, "I'll call Oscar."

She nodded. "Are you able to help me dig a grave?"

"Yes, wait for me." Pieran went to the kitchen and reached up inside one of the cabinets until he found the secure phone. He dialed the doctor and simply said, "Now." He hid the phone again and went back out to Sophie. He couldn't let himself get angry or dissolve into hopelessness. He needed to focus on their goal, which included keeping Sophie from killing herself. Her birthdays were always the worst days.

"You did good," Pieran said softly, stepping up to her. She collapsed into his arms, weeping. He held her and stroked her hair and let her release her anguish.

"This has to stop, Pieran," she sobbed into his chest.

"We're working on it." What was taking their neighboring countries so long? They had plenty of evidence now. One of them had to be compassionate with enough honor and justice to come to their rescue. How many different ways could his network send pleas for help?

Sophie sniffled and trembled. "But what about tomorrow? I can't protect him forever."

That new slave was already lost, but it wasn't the right time to try to help her adjust. "You saved his friend. Be happy about that," Pieran said.

Sophie nodded and pulled back away from him. Her dress was torn, but aside from some humiliation, she wasn't physically wounded. The Prince was still marginally afraid of the King. That was changing and Pieran wouldn't be able to do anything but delay the inevitable once the King was gone.

Pieran pulled the front of her dress closed and said, "Oscar will be here soon. Go change first."

She stumbled back toward her chambers and Pieran went to the kitchen to collect the box they'd prepared the night before. At least there was only one box needed this year. He took it back to the sofa and stared at the tiny kitten with the broken neck and crushed trachea. Its death had been swift, if not painless. Puppies bothered Pieran more, but the Prince knew kittens were one of Sophie's weaknesses.

Gently, he lifted the tiny thing and put it in the box, arranging it to appear to be sleeping on the small blanket there. Its tiny body hadn't stiffened yet and it felt almost like a small bag of beans. He ought to be thankful. This could easily have been that new slave. What had Sophie been thinking to bring that man here? They'd agreed that she would select someone the Prince would find revolting, someone unlikely to be a spy, someone that wouldn't encourage more frequent visits from the Prince.

Sophie returned. She looked like a ghost in the white cotton nightgown, pale and vulnerable. She didn't speak, but instead picked up the box, sighed, and closed the lid. Silently, they went down to her rock garden to the other unmarked graves. Pieran moved several rocks and took the shovel they'd set out and started digging. The hole didn't need to be big or very deep this year.

When he finished digging, Sophie set the box in. "Back to the universe," she intoned softly.

"Into peace," Pieran concluded and filled in the hole. Sophie replaced the rocks. The new grave would be obvious for another week, but then would become part of the landscape, known only to them and the others buried there.

Pieran gazed across the rock garden. The moonlight was bright and lit the ocean of small, white rocks that should easily serve as an aircar landing zone. The meticulously placed, decorative boulders wouldn't interfere with transports, and people could easily step directly onto the lower deck of Sophie's balcony. They couldn't make the invitation more obvious without the King or Prince noticing.

Pieran offered his hand and Sophie took it. She followed him back inside without glancing back. The guards had let the doctor in and they found him with Blair.

"She'll live," Oscar pronounced. "I stitched what I could and I've given her a mild sedative that should wear off by morning."

"Come check the new man," Pieran directed.

The doctor replied, "I saw him on the way in." He turned to Sophie. "You have a choice, Your Highness. I can clean that resin out of the wounds and it'll be painful but he'll have less obvious scars and should heal faster, or I can leave it there and we can hope he doesn't get infected. Who knows what they left underneath."

"Clean him," Sophie said without hesitation. "What do you need?"

"Boiled linens would be best and a trashcan to discard the used ones."

Pieran touched Sophie's arm. "I'll get sheets and cut them down after I start water boiling."

When Pieran returned with supplies, Oscar was in the hallway, silently lecturing Sophie, mouthing the words so the slave wouldn't hear. "You can't mix those two drugs. They're too strong together. It's incredible that you didn't kill him. I can't give him anything else on top of those."

Pieran intercepted this by handing him the steaming pan with material and tongs in it. "Do what you can, Doctor."

"I'll need more than this," Oscar declared, entering the slave's room.

Pieran nodded and went back to start a second batch. He could hear the man's screams. No doubt the guards outside of the suite could also hear them and they'd pass a detailed report to the Prince. Maybe that would be enough to content the Prince for a couple of days?

****

When morning came, Sophie was still sitting on the sofa, staring at the door to the balcony. She'd opened it just about hand-width. It was inviting, that door, hypnotizing, that sliver of unobstructed space. A few simple steps, over the railing, and a jump. Her rocks below would finish this.

But at what cost for her freedom? Pieran and Blair, for sure, and now this man whose name she still didn't know. Perhaps she should give him a name to help him adapt to his new life and forget his old one? Was he one of her brother's spies? Wyatt was certainly capable of arranging that scene in the hallway. Also, Wyatt had barely tormented the man and her brother never held back unless he was planning something exponentially worse.

The balcony door was open, calling to Sophie, beckoning her. Relief. Peace. So very close. All she had to do was stand and walk through that opening.

Pieran entered from the back rooms, strode to the balcony door, and firmly closed it. He turned to Sophie, crossed the room, and sat next to her. Keeping his voice quiet to prevent it from reaching the hallway, he said, "He's awake. He's asking about his friend. I told him I'd check some time today."

Sophie nodded.

Pieran wrapped his arm around her shoulders and pulled her toward him in a supportive hug. "He wanted me to tell his friend that he was ok. Maybe they're brothers. I can't tell if he belongs to Wyatt or not. I'm sorry."

Sophie leaned her head on him. She needed his strength. He'd been at this a lot longer than she had. "We'll have to maintain the pretense then."

"Yeah. I'll go make breakfast." He didn't move.

"How's Blair?" Sophie asked.

"She's been hurt worse. She'll be fine. One day, when this is over, we're going to move far away from here, maybe the Gressuf Mountains. I hear it's pretty. We're going to forget this ever happened and just be husband and wife."

"I think I'd like to go to another country entirely. Maybe work in a bakery."

"You could. You're a good cook."

"Blair's a good teacher."

"Ah, food. Breakfast. What do you want?"

"I'm not eating. I'm not hungry."

He sighed, but didn't argue. He rose and shuffled off to the kitchen.

Sophie looked across the room. The balcony door was closed. It hadn't ever truly been open.

She went to get dressed for the day. She checked on Blair, who was sleeping and snoring softly, and then peered in at her new slave, but the murderous glare he bestowed on her made her retreat to her own chamber with haste.

Sophie was going to have to get that man out before Wyatt could implement whatever he had planned. Pieran wasn't going to endanger the network by sending a third along so soon and he was right. She realized she shouldn't have made him take the risk the day before. If Wyatt or her father found the network, they'd be lost for good and their pain would have been for nothing.

****

Sophie could feel herself languishing under the unrelenting tension of maintaining the illusion that she was a cruel mistress. Her new slave had been up, walking around through the afternoon, with Pieran and Blair showing him his new duties. Sophie stayed on the sofa through most of the day, pretending to read a book, and spent the afternoon rearranging rocks in the yard below her balcony.

By evening, she ached from bending over and couldn't deny her hunger anymore. She went inside, told Blair to bring her food, and ate alone in the dining area. Pieran, Blair, and her new slave stood nearby and watched her eat, ready to get her anything she might want. It would be inappropriate for Sophie to take an interest and ask her new slave's name. She managed to eat about half before she couldn't stand the silence and again went to sit on the sofa.

She left for bed early, but couldn't sleep and lay there, listening to the sounds of her slaves moving about the suite, and thought about how she was going to get rid of her new slave. If he wasn't already owned by her brother, he would be soon and she had to save him from that fate. If he were a spy, it was only a matter of time before she, Pieran, or Blair slipped, and the network would be compromised. It might not be possible to save him. She needed to accept that fact. Pieran would certainly tell her to. They would be safer if she just gave the slave to her brother.

Around midnight, she got up and went outside to stand on the balcony. The early spring air was brisk and the full moon illuminated the rocks below with a tantalizing glowing temptation. She gripped the railing and fantasized about jumping off - a bit of wind in her hair, her nightgown fluttering about her legs, and then nothing. "Back to the universe," she murmured, "Into peace."

Sophie's hands lit from behind and she turned to see her computer light on and her new slave sitting in front of it. He was staring at the passcode screen and shaking his head. In that moment, she knew how she was going to get rid of him. She'd let him escape. She could arrange the opportunity. He might not make it, but there was a chance he would and it was likely his best chance.

Sophie opened the patio door, startling him. He spun around in the chair, eyes wide, obviously terrified to have been caught. Sophie merely said, "The passcode is on a paper in the right hand drawer. My brother monitors everything done on that computer. Don't call anyone you love." She left him, not waiting for a response, and went back to her bed. Her nightmares were a welcome break from her reality.

****

Pieran dreaded this lie, but it was necessary. It was what the Prince had been told that resulted in the Prince taking the entire staff of the furnace pit out into the arena and having them shot. Pieran wasn't going to tell Sophie about that. Maybe she wouldn't find out. One life for eleven would break her heart more than it was already broken. At least they had quick deaths. He wished they could all be so lucky.

Pieran went into the small, plain bedroom where the new slave was sleeping. It was still pre-dawn and he wanted to know how dangerous this man was going to be before Sophie was awake. Pieran tapped the man on his shoulder, waking him. Pieran put his finger over his mouth telling the man to be quiet.

Pieran whispered, "I was able to check on your friend last night. I'm sorry, but he tripped and fell into the furnace. He didn't make it."

The man winced, closed his eyes, and shook in obvious anguish. "Tripped or was pushed?" he hissed softly, opening his eyes again.

"In this miserable abyss, I'm not sure there's a difference. I'm really sorry." Pieran repeated his apology and went outside, standing in the hallway listening. He heard the new slave roll out of his bed and heard him quietly sobbing. Satisfied the man wouldn't go into an immediate violent rage, Pieran went to Sophie's room and sat down in one of her chairs to watch her sleep and protect her if the man decided to retaliate.

Dawn came with chilly sunlight rays through the delicate curtains at the window. Pieran yawned as Sophie stirred, groaning and rubbing at her temples. She saw Pieran. "What is it?" she asked. She swallowed.

Pieran raised his hand and gestured that it was nothing urgent. "The man you ordered to the furnace pit fell into the furnace and died. I told your new slave this morning." Their voices would carry down the hall. The suite was too small for privacy.

Sophie sat up. "I let him use the computer last night."

Pieran frowned and rolled his eyes. She needed to be smarter. What would the Prince do with the knowledge that she allowed her slaves free access to the computer?

Sophie shrugged. "I want to shop for a new dress today - replace the one that got torn."

Pieran really frowned then. He mouthed, "No." at her and shook his head.

"Go wake the others and arrange transport. I want to leave as soon as breakfast is over, before it gets too warm and the sun rises enough to damage my skin." She swung her legs over the side of the bed. "I may also buy some furniture. Might as well make use of the strength of my new slave."

"Of course, Your Highness." He made a disgruntled face at her and went to do as bid. Maybe she needed to know about the furnace pit staff? Decisions had consequences.

Pieran went to Blair first. She was already pulling on her clothes. "I heard," she said. "It's not supposed to rain today."

Pieran nodded and went to their new slave's room. "We're going to the market," he announced. The man's eyes were red. "I'll change your bandages. The doctor left some cream."

"Thank you. I'd appreciate the help," the man said. "I was just wondering how I was going to do that." As Pieran was applying the antibiotic pain medicine, the man asked, "Which town are we going to?"

"Risell. It's just outside of the castle. There's a fairly big market, but mostly local goods." Pieran continued to describe it. He wouldn't ask if the man was familiar with Risell because the less anyone knew about the man, the safer his family and friends would be.

They finished and went to get breakfast. They ate with Blair in the kitchen. Blair took the opportunity to also express her condolences. They served Sophie in the dining area but she frowned at the meal and said she wasn't hungry, and she instructed Pieran to bring extra money for furniture. At that directive, Pieran guessed what Sophie had in mind. It was risky. They couldn't use the network, but maybe the man could save himself.

They took a groundcar over to Risell, escorted by two watchful guards that belonged to the Prince. They walked from the parking area across the cobblestone streets because the paths had been designed for horseback and carts and were too narrow for vehicle traffic. Most of the buildings were made from worn blocks of stone and had greenery growing on them. The town might have been pleasantly charming if the gaunt townsfolk didn't scurry out of their way, dodging fearfully into buildings.

The center market area was more open, but even in this wealthier part of the country, many of the vendors had temporary structures that weren't well-stocked. There were a few scattered tables where people might eat. Shoppers, seeing the small entourage, quickly vacated the area, without appearing to rush, obviously not wanting to draw any attention to themselves. Merchants shuffled about, rearranging their displays and looking busy.

Sophie went directly to the dress shop. She stopped outside and said, "Pieran, I'm hungry after all. Take him," she gestured at her new slave, "And show him where the best foods are."

One of the guards spoke up, "Your Highness, one of us should go with them."

"If you insist, but you will explain to my brother why you left me unprotected." Sophie shrugged and strode into the store. Blair followed.

The second guard said, "I'll stand out here. You go in with them."

The first guard glanced at Pieran unhappily and entered the shop.

Pieran touched the slave's arm and said, "Come on. I know where everything is. I'll show you around. You may need to come here on your own one day to make a purchase."

As soon as they were out of the guard's sight, Pieran stopped. "Oh! I need to arrange next week's food delivery. Here, take this." He shoved the bag of paper money and coins at the man. "Follow that path until you see the kabob place. She likes the lamb and vegetable one, but bring one of each in case she's feeling ornery. I'll meet you back here." Pieran walked off purposefully in a different direction. The kabobs wouldn't be nearly done this early in the day, so even if he were too stupid to realize his good fortune, he'd have time to figure it out while waiting.

Pieran stopped at every shop along the path, not staying long at any of them. He looked over the products and did not engage in conversations. The network people touched their eyebrows in a subtle salute, but didn't engage. An older woman approached him as he was perusing a potato cart.

"He's asking for a phone," she said, selecting two sweet potatoes and paying for them.

"Give him a secure line," Pieran replied and moved on to the next stall. The woman ambled back in the other direction. This was absurd. The idiot should have been gone by now.

Pieran stopped at the coal seller, who gave him the modified salute. "Any problems with the last delivery?"

"None that I'm aware of. Should reach its destination sometime next week."

"Excellent. Coal is critical these days."

"Not so much over the summer. You have a good day, Sir."

Pieran smiled his thanks and went onward. Three booths later, he discreetly delivered yet another letter to be sent to one of the neighboring countries. This one had more pictures from inside the dungeons, taken from a man (now dead) who monitored security feeds. It was yet another plea for justice on behalf of the innocents. He circled back, at the same steady, slow pace, visiting each shop.

Pieran nearly swore out loud when he saw the man waiting with a bag of kabobs. They'd have to destroy whatever secure line had been used. It wasn't secure anymore. There was only one possibility; the man was one of the Prince's creatures. If Sophie had compromised the network, they were lost.

Chapter 2

Blair ran her fingers across the small sample of velvety suede. One day, she might like a robe made of this creamy softness. It would be warm and easy to snuggle into. Dreams kept her sane.

The guard shifted his feet uncomfortably, but was ignored. Across the warm, claustrophobic room stacked with material samples, Sophie was yet again lamenting how the last dress had grown too tight across her bosom and how she'd likely need a completely new wardrobe by the end of the year. Madame Violet, the seamstress, was agreeing and happily discussing differences in support systems, shapes, and necklines.

As the point was to drag out the fitting as long as possible to give Pieran time to do whatever he needed, Blair asked a question every so often that would spawn another round of discussions. Each time, the guard glared at her. He was sweltering, dripping sweat in his heavy body armor. The sun was shining inside through the window and even without the added bodies, the room would have been hot.

Sophie's stomach rumbled. "My slaves should be back with food by now."

Madame Violet gasped. "Oh, Your Highness, I'm sorry. I've kept you too long. I have your measurements and I'll bring you a dress before the end of the week."

Sophie tilted her head regally and, without even saying goodbye or thank you, stepped out of the shop into the late morning sunlight.

Blair followed, blinking in the brightness. She scanned the market and saw Pieran and the new slave across the courtyard at a table under a tent. Blair cringed. Hadn't Pieron grasped that he was supposed to help the man escape?

"They're over there, Your Highness," Blair offered, pointing.

Sophie held up her hand and shaded her eyes, squinting in that direction. Without a word, she marched over to the table. Pieran immediately stood and nudged the man to stand also.

"Kabobs, Your Highness," Pieran said, lifting the bag from the table and passing it to Blair.

Sophie sat down and looked expectantly at Blair.

Blair quickly emptied the bag, sorting through the contents. The vendor had included metal silverware and extra napkins, as well as a real plate. She arranged the place setting and stepped back deferentially, taking a place next to Pieran. The guards positioned themselves at either end of the table, gazing out over the empty courtyard.

Sophie picked through the meat and vegetables, selectively choosing bits and taking her time to cut and eat it.

Midway through the meal, a young girl came over carrying a pink flower on a long stem. She curtseyed low and said timidly, "A flower for you, Your Highness." She set the flower on the table next to Sophie and ran off. Sophie sighed and brushed the flower off the table. It fell to the ground. "Must they always interrupt my meal?"

Blair hoped the ritual looked callous enough to the guards. The next child to be shipped to the Wallace Lords and to safety sometimes gave her a single flower, knowing that she couldn't accept it, acknowledge it, or in any way appreciate it. It was the town's way of showing their thanks for everything Sophie did to try and keep them safe.

When Sophie finished eating, she stood up, deliberately stepping on and crushing the flower. "Furniture is next."

"I'll stay and clean this up, Your Highness," Blair volunteered. She wanted to go back to ask Madame Violet if their new slave's friend had been extracted safely.

"Leave it. One of these idle shopkeepers can take care of it." Sophie led them down the cobblestone streets, stopping at whatever interested her. She pointed at things, and Pieran paid for them, and they were given to the new slave to carry.

Several times, Pieran and the new slave were sent to drop things off at the car. They both always returned. Eventually, Sophie found a polished wooden end table that she said she liked and she declared the shopping done.

They rode back in silence. The suite's door was open.

They found the Prince sitting on the sofa with his feet propped up. He saw them at the doorway and stood. "Sister, it's about time you returned. I've been done with the second half of your birthday present for hours."

He stood aside to let them enter the room. Blair kept her eyes downcast, screaming inside. He shouldn't be here again already!

Out of the corner of her eye, Blair saw Sophie lean in and kiss her brother on the cheek. Sophie sang, "What did you bring me, Your Highness? Last night's gifts were already generous."

"You'll see. You'll love it." He laughed and pointed toward the balcony door.

Sophie walked over to it and gasped, stopping and jerking as if slapped.

The Prince giggled maniacally and crossed the room to stand next to her. "Isn't it magnificent, Sophie?"

"You've outdone yourself, Your Highness," she replied quietly.

"You should kiss my feet in gratitude." He paused. "Well, maybe not you. That's not very dignified for a Princess."

Sophie pointed at Blair. "Kiss his boots."

Blair moved to obey, knowing he'd probably kick her in the face. She understood why Sophie had chosen her. While the Prince enjoyed both men and women, he preferred women.

"No," the Prince said sharply. "The new one. I want to know if your training measures were effective. I'd be remiss in my brotherly duties if I didn't offer you my experience in such matters."

Blair stepped back, trying not to attract the Prince's attention that was now riveted on the new slave.

One of the Prince's guards has the gall to snicker.

The new slave paled and stiffened. Blair silently begged him to do it. His next stop was a dungeon if he didn't. After a split second that seemed to last an eternity, the new slave stepped forward, and with dignity, dropped to his knees and kissed the Prince's boots. The Prince stroked his hair as if he were a pet and then grabbed his hair and jerked upwards. When the slave's face was facing the him, the Prince said, "Next time, don't be so slow, slave." The Prince kicked the man in the chest, sending him sprawling backwards across the floor. The man gasped as the floor smashed against his welts from the whipping.

The Prince turned to Sophie, "I'll come by tomorrow to see if you've managed to teach him speedier obedience. Meanwhile, enjoy your new present." He laughed, hugged her, and skipped away, bouncing happily.

The Prince's trap was clear. He'd come back daily, until the new slave failed one of his tests, and the slave would be taken to the dungeon for training and likely never be seen again. Dead or not, they'd be told he was dead.

Pieran, after a moment, followed the Prince. He would make sure the Prince was actually gone.

Blair was torn between looking out of the window and tending to the man who was now wincing and trying to roll over.

Sophie went over to the glass door and slid to her knees in front of it, resting her head on the glass. Her shoulders shook in silent sobs.

Blair chose the man. "Here, let me help," she said, trying to assist him without hurting him. She pulled. He was even heavier than she'd thought. It was that dense muscle. He was rock solid. He managed to get an arm under himself and pushed himself up. There was blood visible through the back of his shirt and a bright red stain on the carpet. He shook his head at her offer of more assistance and sat there breathing hard.

Blair went over to Sophie. Outside, the rock garden had been replaced with soft, squishy loam with small fruit trees and bushes. It had been landscaped to have a small hill and stream with a pond. It was gorgeous and entirely unacceptable as an aircar landing pad for their potential rescuers. Sophie glanced up at Blair, tears openly rolling down her cheeks.

Until Pieran had a chance to sweep the suite for bugs and surveillance cameras, they had to assume the Prince was watching them. Blair took a knee and bowed her head, "What would you like me to do, Your Highness?"

Sophie finally seemed to focus. She nodded toward the man. "Get that cleaned up."

Blair climbed to her feet, offered a hand to Sophie, who didn't take it, but stood herself. Sophie walked like a zombie toward her bedroom.

Blair went over to the man. "Come on, I'll fix your bandages."

He sighed and with obviously pained effort, managed to stand.

Sophie's scream echoed down the hallway. Blair ran toward it. Sophie continued to wail loudly.

Blair got to Sophie's chamber, pushed past Sophie who was standing in the doorway, and threw her hand over her own mouth to keep from throwing up. The Prince had dug up over a decade of dead animals and arranged what remained of them on Sophie's bed. This year's kitten was curled on her pillow. Maggots were already crawling over it.

Blair grabbed Sophie and pulled her away. She didn't care about the potential cameras. She took the girl back to her own room and set her on the bed. "Stay here, Your Highness. I'll take care of it."

****

Pieran finished sweeping the suite for electronics for the third time. He'd gotten the dead animals out expediently by just wrapping them in the bedding and carrying the bundle away. The smell hadn't been as bad as it could have been, but he had opened all of the windows anyway.

As nearly as he could tell, he'd gotten the cameras and microphones out. The only things still registering as electronics were the computer, the phone, and his secure phone. He even pulled apart the computer to be certain that wasn't tampered with.

Sophie was still sitting on Blair's bed, almost catatonic. Blair had fixed the man's bandages and scrubbed the blood from the carpet with a heavy amount of salt and was now on the main phone, calling contractors to restore the rock garden. The slave, as directed by Blair, was laying on his bed, trying not to move and aggravate his wounds.

Pieran rubbed at his neck and went to Sophie. "The suite's clean," he announced softly.

"I want that bed replaced."

"We'll get it done tomorrow. Stay in here tonight, Your Highness. Blair can bunk with me."

"I want the rocks back."

"Blair's calling contractors. We should be able to have it reset by the end of the week."

"Tonight. I want it finished tonight."

"It's already late, Your Highness."

"I'll help." The unexpected voice from the doorway made Pieran spin around. The new slave was standing, shirtless and shimmering, in the doorway. The tape holding the bandages to his back was visible along his sides. A boot-shaped bruise was forming across the man's sternum.

Pieran crossed the short distance to stand nose-to-nose with the man. "You," Pieran growled, "Will do precisely as you're told, immediately and without hesitation or attitude, no matter what that is. Go back to your room and lay down."

"No," Sophie cut in. "If he wants to help, he can help. I want it done tonight."

Pieran shook his head. "But Your Highness, it's unreasonable."

"I don't believe I asked for your opinion, slave." Sophie got up. "I'm going to go change. We have a lot of work ahead of us."

Pieran bit his lip. They were going to need rest if they were going to survive the Prince's visit the following day. Fixing the rock garden was going to take most of the night if they could even get contractors. They didn't have the hours or the physical stamina they'd need. Pieran sighed and stepped out of Sophie's way. He glared at their new slave, who glared back.

Pieran went to see how Blair was doing with finding contractors, ignoring the new slave.

Blair had just disconnected. She said, "I found someone willing to come out within the hour and tear out the vegetation and level it. She wants it done tonight, doesn't she?"

Pieran sighed. "Yes. You're wiser than me."

"He doesn't have any rocks though. If we can find some, he says he'll spread them out. They won't be completely stable until they settle, but it should work well enough and get a good start on it. It's not like people are rushing to experience the joy of a rock garden anyway."

Pieran hugged her and rested his head on hers. "Oh, love. I'm so tired. I'm so tired of all of this." Ever so quietly, he breathed into her ear, "He wouldn't go."

"Shhh, love." She stroked his back, holding him tightly. "This is a day, just like any other. We get through today and worry about tomorrow, tomorrow."

Pieran sighed, straightening. "He had to throw the rocks away somewhere. Can we find them?"

"Trash would certainly be cheaper than new rocks." Blair kissed him and pushed him away so she could get back to the phone.

****

Grayson's fingers were bleeding. Shoot, his back was bleeding. He could feel it dripping, mingling with sweat. He'd never hurt so much in his life. As much as he physically hurt, emotionally he was still numb. He'd gotten Finn killed. His bodyguard, sure, but also his best friend. They were only meant to do a simple recon - ask about the rumors, find out the situation, and bring back trustworthy proof if they could.

Somehow, Grayson and Finn had attracted attention and were ambushed and picked up. The men had brought them to the castle guards and now he was busy being thankful that monster Princess was insane and demanding the rock garden be restored.

His frantic phone call to his father in the marketplace was the first bit of luck he'd had since entering this reprehensible country. His father had told him to stay and that they would send troops. While the people he'd petitioned about the injustices here weren't willing to invade on a rumor, they apparently could justify it to rescue someone of his lineage.

Grayson went back to the pile for another bucket of rocks. The bulldozers had spread the initial layers, but it needed more to be stable. It was still precarious and they could expect to loose some landing gear on the unstable surface.

Grayson paused briefly to look up at the moon to try and judge the time. His father's army, along with troops from several of their neighbors, would arrive at 3 a.m. local time, whether or not they had a landing zone, and he'd just told them to come here. The crazy woman's rock garden had been the perfect spot with full access to the castle.

Grayson had seen enough to know the truth was worse than the rumors. He had hazy memories of the Prince's visit, but what he did recall, he wished he couldn't. Human decency required action. These people needed to be rescued and it wasn't just the slaves in the castle that needed their help.

The local news media praised the King and royal family and proclaimed the riches of the citizens, but the people were cautious, reserved, and utterly terrified of anyone they didn't recognize. Many were starving. While the country's media and surveillance systems were modern, their overall technology and wealth were pitiful. Most had electricity, but they didn't have aircars and few had groundcars. Private transportation was by foot, bicycle, or horse-drawn cart.

The woman slave appeared at his side with a large glass of water. "Drink," she said.

"Is it drugged this time?" he asked directly and watched her response. One day he wanted to find out why she was trying to drug the Princess with the Prince so soon to arrive. That had been sheer stupidity, but neither servant had even bothered to ask his name. They weren't friendly enough for him to consider conversation with and certainly not such an inquiry.

"No. It's got some lemon and a tiny bit of salt in it to replace your electrolytes." She held the glass out and he took it.

Grayson sniffed it but wasn't sure if he'd recognize drugs anyway. Could he trust her? He swore to himself. He was thirsty. He drank it and wished he had another one.

"I'm going to make sandwiches and try to get Her Highness to eat. What would you like on yours?"

"Anything but vegetables."

"I'd get you something for the pain, but we have limited medical supplies. We have to save them for when they're really needed.

You're hurt but you aren't immobile. I'll fix your bandages again when we're done."

Grayson nodded and looked over to where the crazy Princess was pushing more rocks around with her foot. "I don't want them anyway."

The woman took the empty glass from him and said, "I don't know why you're helping right now, but thank you. The rock garden means a lot to her."

Grayson didn't answer that and turned to the rock pile and tried to scoop more rocks into his bucket without adding more cuts to his hands. He was focusing his efforts on the area right next to the lower deck of the balcony. They each seemed to be taking different areas of the garden, which suited him just fine. They'd need places for multiple ships to land.

Pieran arrived with his bucket just as Grayson finished loading his. The older man looked flushed and winded and was moving even slower than he'd been when they started. How did they endure this torture?

"Why don't you take a break?" Grayson said.

"Why don't you?" the old man retorted.

****

Sophie wiped her bloody hands on her shirt and took the empty bucket back to the pile. The sandwich Blair had forced her to eat had long since been used up and her stomach growled. She was dizzy as she stumbled across the uneven rocks. Had her brother known the reason for the rock garden or was he simply destroying something she apparently loved? She desperately hoped for the later.

Blair came over to her and pointed at Pieran. Pieran wobbled, barely able to stand, as he dumped his bucket. "It's enough for the night, Your Highness. We can hire more contractors after sunrise to finish this layer and make it more solid." Blair, who had taken breaks and organized the contractors until they departed, had more energy than the rest of them.

Sophie nodded, defeated. She was stumbling more than walking. She couldn't say who would fall first - her or Pieran. "Is it truly enough?" She wiped sweat from her forehead and eyes.

"Yes, Your Highness."

Even out here, they were maintaining the pretense. Could her new slave even hear from that far away? "Ok, tell them we're done for the night. Go help Pieran."

"Yes, Your Highness." She curtsied and shuffled off wearily.

Sophie nearly tripped as she made her way to the staircase to the lower deck. Her muscles protested the climb, but she managed to get back to the suite. She crossed the main room and dropped onto the sofa. She was too drained and exhausted to make it to Blair's bed. Blair and Pieran arrived, followed almost immediately by her new slave.

Blair helped Pieran sit on one of the chairs and turned to the new slave. "Come on, I'll clean your back and change your bandages."

He nodded tiredly, "What time is it?"

Blair shrugged and started back toward the hallway. He followed.

Sophie's head was spinning and she closed her eyes. She could rest for just a moment...

A shadow passing over her eyes woke her and her eyes fluttered open in time to see a strange man in full black military combat gear leaning over her. He shoved a thick cloth into her mouth and slapped a piece of tape over it and proceeded to efficiently wrap tape around her wrists and ankles. Across the room, Sophie saw Pieran was already similarly bound. Other men dressed in the same black outfits were silently pouring into the room through the balcony door.

She heard a gasp by the hallway and saw Blair. Blair was holding her new slave by the elbow to help him walk. His hair was damp and he was in fresh clothes. Sophie squinted at them groggily, bewilderingly wondering why they hadn't gone to sleep.

One of the men in black threw a dagger which lodged in Blair's throat and she trembled for a moment, gurgling, before sliding gracefully to the floor. Her slave frowned down at the body, but stepped over it. Silently, he held up two fingers and pointed toward the suite's front door.

Several of the men went and efficiently, quietly, killed the two guards outside of the door and pulled their bodies into the suite.

Her slave whispered to one of the men, "The back rooms are empty. Is it 3 already?"

"Yes, Milord. After, actually. We had some problems landing. I thought you said..."

Her slave cut him off with a quick hand gesture. "It doesn't matter. Get these two out of here. That one's the Princess." He pointed at Sophie.

Men immediately moved to obey. Sophie swirled with vertigo as they picked her up and efficiently carried her through the balcony door just behind the men with Pieran. The night air was cold and she shivered. They were lowered onto the floor of some sort of transport vehicle and Pieran fell against her. The men told the pilot to watch them and then went back inside. The pilot stared at them for a few minutes until a radio beeped behind him. He turned to answer it, and

Pieran shifted until his hands were against Sophie's. Pieran rapidly tapped her fingers with his own and Sophie finally began to grasp what was happening. She was simply too exhausted to think clearly. She forced herself to peel the tape from his wrists.

Freed, he ripped the tape from her hands and feet and pointed toward the door. When she didn't move quickly enough, he pulled the tape from his own mouth. "Get out of here! Run!" He shoved her toward the vehicle's door and threw himself at the pilot who'd turned at the sound.

Sophie did, sprinting out of the vehicle. She bounced off of a man on the landing, who, startled, was unable to stop her as she launched herself over the staircase railing. She ran.

Sophie was halfway to Risell before she collapsed. She glanced back toward the castle to see a flash of light. This was followed almost immediately by the sound of the explosion. She could hear the gunfire then. A siren sounded. She peeled the tape off of her mouth, spitting out the cloth and inhaled deeply. She needed to get to the network. She had to send the passcodes for the dungeons or whoever that was would kill the occupants trying to get in.

Sophie struggled to her knees and then stood and hobbled onward. When she finally got to the cobblestone, she caught her foot on a stone and fell to her knees. One of the vendors, up early and pulling a cart of wares, saw Sophie, gasped, and rushed over.

"Madame Violet," Sophie said, "Get me to her."

The woman nodded and grabbed Sophie's arm, wrapping it over her own shoulders. She mostly carried Sophie to the dressmaker's shop.

****

Outside of Madame Violet's shop, Sophie leaned on the woman, waiting. The chilly air seeped through to her bones, causing her to shiver. It seemed to take forever for Madame Violet to answer. She was still pulling her robe closed as she opened the shop door. She saw Sophie and quickly yanked them inside.

"It's happening," Sophie wheezed. "Invasion at the castle. We have to get them the passcodes."

"We have to get you out of here, Your Highness." Madame Violet called over her shoulder, "Noah! Wake up. I need you!" She directed the shopkeeper to go back to her routine as if nothing were amiss. The woman hastened off without hesitation. Madame Violet led Sophie to her kitchen and started digging in the drawers.

Madame Violet's son appeared, rubbing at his eyes. He was maybe 15 years old. He should have already been with the Wallace Lords. It was too dangerous for him to still be here. His mouth dropped open when he saw Sophie.

Madame Violet said, "You remember the pickup number, Noah?" He nodded. "Go call it for her and come back." Noah left. To Sophie, Madame Violet said, "Are you hurt?"

Sophie shook her head. She was, but it didn't matter.

"Ok, I'm going to cut your hair. We need to make you look different. Get out of those clothes." The woman sped this along by pulling on Sophie's shirt, swiftly and efficiently helping her undress.

Noah arrived. "They said 10 minutes, out the back tunnel."

Sophie said, "I need paper and pen. And someone to take the passcodes back to the castle or the people in the dungeons will die."

"I can do it," Noah offered.

"No," his mother replied sharply. "Go fetch some of my clothes upstairs. Quickly now, something dark and plain."

Noah dashed off.

Madame Violet was already cutting Sophie's hair and dropping the long locks into a pot on her stove. Noah returned shortly with a selection of clothes, which Madame Violet dug through and passed her choices to Sophie to put on. Noah left and came back again and put a notepad and pen in front of Sophie. Sophie nodded her thanks and as Madame Violet finished cutting, Sophie wrote down the dungeon locations and passcodes so expensively acquired and meticulously memorized. She tore off the page and Madame Violet took the remainder of the notepad and tore the rest of the pages and threw them into the pot with Sophie's hair. She took a match and lit it. Then she took a broom and swept up the strands of fallen hair. She added that to the flames, too.

Noah picked up the list and read it. "They won't shoot a kid and I'm fast."

"Noah, no!" his mother objected, reaching for him, but the boy had already darted out of the kitchen, clutching the paper in a closed fist. They heard the bell on the shop's front door a split second later.

Sophie put her hand on Madame Violet's. "He's right. They wont hurt him." They better not hurt him.

His mother whimpered, "My son!" She shook her head. "I'm going to thrash him until he can't sit for a week when he gets back." She growled angrily and then sighed. "We have to get you to the pickup point. Come on."

She led Sophie through the back hallway to the bathroom and lifted the rug. The trapdoor was next, and Sophie climbed down into the darkness. Madame Violet followed. Once the trapdoor was shut,

Madame Violet flipped a switch and a series of lights lit a tunnel. "This way," the woman directed.

At one point, Sophie careened dizzily into the wall, and Madame Violet caught her and practically carried her the rest of the way. They passed several side tunnels but continued straight. They reached a ladder at the end and waited.

"Do you really think Noah will be ok?" Madame Violet's voice wavered.

"Yes." Sophie had no idea.

"Was it really an invasion? Is it over?"

By 'over', Sophie knew Madame Violet meant the dungeons, not the invasion, but she couldn't offer hope. She said, "They had enough troops to take the castle. I saw more ships coming in as I was on my way here." She didn't mention that it seemed to be spearheaded by her new slave.

The trapdoor above them lifted and a man peered in. "Come on," he said.

Sophie climbed, ignoring the pain in her hands, knees, and feet, that were starting to scream as her adrenaline waned. Her foot slipped once and Madame Violet caught it from below and pushed upwards.

The man helped Sophie the rest of the way and then shut the trapdoor on Madame Violet with a nod. He practically carried Sophie to the waiting groundcar and put her in the back seat where another woman waited.

That woman said, "The caller indicated you needed medical. Tell me what's hurt."

****

Finn hit the wall with frustration. He was locked in another basement room. There was a bed, food, a sink with items for washing, and yet another change of clothing.

These people were infuriating. He needed a phone, not a sink. He needed to call home and tell them to rescue Grayson. It had been nearly two weeks since he'd been rushed out of the furnace pit by two cloaked individuals. Who knew what those psychopaths were doing to Grayson? If those pictures from the supposed dungeons were real and not faked...

Finn had been escorted to over fifteen locations now, mostly by people wearing full face masks who refused to speak to him. The ones that did talk to him kept repeating that he was a safe and was on his way to somewhere that he could stay a while. One of them had even been so verbose as to say that she couldn't give him a phone because any calls put them in danger and then she had refused to say anything else.

He went over to the sink and washed and changed. Then he ate. He had no complaints about their treatment, really. He knew the people of this country were pathetically poor. These arrangements would be considered a feast. If only they would listen to him...

There was a knock at the door and then he heard the outside bolt move.

"Are you dressed?" a woman's voice asked politely. Another new person. He hadn't seen the same person twice.

When he said he was, the woman entered. She was wearing a shroud that obscured her features.

"May we talk?" Her voice sounded like it was going through a modulator of some sort.

"Of course." He would love to talk.

"You aren't a prisoner," she said.

"The locked door suggests otherwise."

"Yes, for your own safety and for the safety of the people who live here." She opened the door and brought in a chair which she proceeded to sit on. "Please," she indicated that he should sit on the bed and he did. "I'm told you are adamant about contacting your home."

"Yes, I need to call them. Do you have a phone I can use?" Finn held his breath.

"I have a secure phone, but the problem is that whoever you call will not have a secure phone. Your voice will have been registered on the monitoring lists from the moment you were taken from the castle. Whoever you call will be picked up and punished for your escape. You have to let them go and be satisfied with the knowledge that you're protecting them."

Finn groaned and tried to explain, "That's not a problem. I need to call outside of the country."

"That's worse. Communications that leave here will be traced back to its source and then, even the secure line wouldn't have been secure enough." Her hand rubbed at her knee in an unconscious gesture. "Do you realize how lucky you are to be here right now?"

"Yes, and I thank you for that, but my friend is still back there."

"Ah, I understand now. I'm sorry. There's nothing you can do for... him or her?"

"Him." Finn bit his lip, trying to keep from strangling her out of frustration. "How do you normally communicate outside of the country?"

"You must realize I can't answer that. My job today was to evaluate where you'd be best placed for a permanent home, you see, to find somewhere compatible. We didn't know you had foreign family."

"Because no one would talk to me."

"Security protocol. They weren't allowed. If you get picked up again, we don't want you to be able to identify any of us. You are a foreigner?" She tilted her head and then continued, "That would explain why you don't grasp the severity of your situation, but it does make my task easier. I don't have to find you somewhere to live. What country are you from?"

Finn wondered if he should answer that. What could they possibly do to him or his home? "Demense. I'm from Demense."

She nodded. "Very well. We'll take you there, but we need you to cooperate. Stop hounding the couriers about phones and stop talking. Don't draw any attention to yourself. These people are putting their lives and that of their family at risk for you." She stood.

Finn also stood. "Tell me something," he said, seizing the opportunity. "I saw pictures from inside a dungeon. Are they real?"

The woman stiffened and then answered, "Yes, but they're only from the least secure locations. The inner dungeons are worse than anything shown. We haven't been able to get footage of that yet. You'd have been in one if we hadn't pulled you out. Why would you ever come to our country?"

"I came with my friend."

"I'm truly sorry. We can't help him." She left, locking the door again.

Finn leaned on the wall. Would they really take him to Demense? How long would it take?

****

"We're here," the driver said. "You can sit up."

Sophie stretched, as much as she could on the floor of the vehicle, waking her stiff, cramped muscles. She pulled herself up onto the groundcar's back seat. The midmorning sun cast a warm yellow light across a field of flowers, beyond which could be seen a fenced area with cows and a barn. Another fenced field had three horses peacefully eating grass. Farther down the dirt driveway, there was a small, wooden farmhouse atop a gentle, sloping hill. In the distance, Sophie could see mountains. The dirt driveway curved in front of the house, forming a loop.

Sophie hadn't even know her country had such a place in it. Had Pieran prearranged for this obviously affluent place to be her refuge? What was happening to Pieran? She couldn't let herself think about Blair yet.

The car stopped directly in front of the door. "Good luck, miss," he said.

"Thank you." Sophie got out of the vehicle and the groundcar started moving as soon as its door closed. She stood in the driveway and watched until the groundcar disappeared. She felt unsettled, standing alone in unfamiliar clothes, about to impose upon complete strangers.

The front door of the house opened and an old woman said, "Come in, pet. Don't be shy."

Just inside, an open sitting room had multiple chairs, including two rocking chairs, and a lit fireplace. Toward the back, there was a small dining table that would seat four. Lovely handmade crafts constructed from various fibers decorated the walls. A beautiful floral quilt hung opposite the fireplace.

An old man was waiting. He came forward with a smile and held out his hands. Sophie took took them, squeezing in the traditional greeting, and the man said, "Welcome to our home, miss. I'm Raymond and this is my wife Marie."

Sophie didn't answer with her own name. It was against the security protocols. She was to be given a new name.

"We've made breakfast for you," the woman said. "Come sit at the table. We have a packet of information for you from the network. Can you read?"

Sophie nodded and said, "Thank you for taking me in." She hoped that packet had information about the invasion. She'd been transferred and moved several times and had spent entirely too long in an empty basement. The network wasn't taking any chances of her being spotted or found, but she needed to know what was going on. Had the invasion been successful? Were the King and Prince finally dead? Security protocol dictated that she wasn't allowed to talk with anyone until she reached her final destination. "It's very kind of you."

Marie smiled warmly. "Oh, it's no trouble, pet. We were surprised to finally get called. We've been registered as a safe house for years."

Sophie tried to return the smile. She didn't really know how and her facial muscles twitched uncertainly. "Is there any news from the castle?"

"Are you her? Princess Sophie?" Raymond asked.

Sophie nodded. It was probably better if they knew. They needed to be given a chance to turn her out. Her presence put them in danger.

"There are rumors," he said. "Out here, we don't get much news from Risell. Can't trust anything on the media. Was there really an invasion?"

"Yes. I'm not sure who it was, though. I was hoping you'd know. Did they succeed?"

He shook his head. "We don't know."

"Well," Marie said, taking Sophie's elbow and steering her toward the table. "Let's not worry about that right now, pet. You have breakfast to eat and an information packet to go through."

There was a folder on the table. Sophie sat in front of it and opened it. Pages of handwritten notes about her new identity, where "Gail" was from, her family, relatives, information about farming, things she should know about the town where she'd grown up. Names of pets, friends. Were these real people? Would they say they knew a Gail if asked? How thorough was Pieran's network?

Marie set a plate of food next to her. Eggs, biscuits, jam, butter, on a delicate floral plate. "Tea, milk, or fruit juice?" she inquired.

"I don't expect you to serve me," Sophie said gently. "Let me help around the house. Teach me what needs to be done to help you with the farm. I'm good at baking and I'm able to cook. I don't mind cleaning. I don't want to be a burden."

"Tomorrow's soon enough for that, pet. Rest today. Settle in. We're going to have to adjust your clothes to fit you right. That'll be enough for today."

****

Grayson sat on the edge of King's bed and rubbed at his eyes. The room had been completely cleaned and sanitized and the offensive appointments had been removed, but he still found it repulsive. The whole castle was repulsive.

This was hell. They should have come to these people's rescue as soon as the reports started appearing. He'd thought a couple days with the Princess was bad. That was a vacation compared to what they'd found in the dungeons.

There'd been no survivors from those. Without the passcodes, electronics activated bombs and traps that killed the occupants indiscriminately, as if to say, 'if we can't have them, you can't either'. Dungeon cells remained intact enough to advertise the horrors bestowed on the unfortunate people there. They'd found five such dungeons already and he wouldn't be surprised if they were missing a few, with the occupants slowly starving to death. He had people looking, desperately looking.

The King was dead, but both the Princess and Prince had escaped. He had people searching for them, too. The other lords of Demense were sending support troops, but it would take them a while to arrive and integrate with the troops already here. None of the local staff could be trusted. The ones that weren't demented into fanatical devotion to the royals were actively terrified of the Prince and Princess coming back. The fanatics were trying to kill him and his people while the others were unwilling to be seen helping him.

The castle was in ruins. Most of the food had been poisoned. The water stores had been contaminated and water from the nearby river had to be boiled to be potable. The smell of the funeral pyres permeated everything and he was having a problem getting his own staff to clear bodies out of the dungeons. No one wanted to go in and most of those that did refused to go back a second time. Of those, many were so traumatized by the experience that they could no longer function in their duties and had to be sent home for counseling.

He'd begged neighboring countries to provide humanitarian aid, but they were refusing to come in until 'the domestic disturbance' was over and he could guarantee their safety. The country's news media was actively suppressing the truth, presumably out of fear of the royals, and he didn't have the troops to take over those information centers yet.

As if that weren't enough, parts of his back were infected. His doctor had him on a strict regimen of antibiotics and mandatory medical treatments multiple times per day. He ached everywhere. He'd sprained his ankle sometime during the rearrangement of the rocks the night of his rescue, and he simply didn't have the time to 'stay seated and keep it elevated with ice on it' per the doctor's orders.

It was an unholy mess and friend and foe alike were demanding he be responsible for cleaning it up. They came to him for orders and expected him to have answers for everything.

He couldn't focus. He couldn't get the images of those tortured and mutilated bodies out of his head. They should have come sooner. Why had he taken so long to come himself? These people needed to be rescued from the royals. He'd failed those poor souls and guilt threatened to overwhelm him.

Chapter 3

The morning sun shone through the cracks in the barn's woodwork, illuminating the hay with a rich, golden light. Sophie stood paralyzed, transfixed by the mother cat and her pile of squirming kittens. She'd been sent to the barn to get a pitchfork for Raymond, but she hadn't expected to see kittens. She was unreasonably terrified of them, afraid she'd kill them by her mere presence.

"Cute, aren't they?" a girl's voice said behind her.

Sophie jumped.

"Mommy says I can have one this year. I'm Adele." She held out her hands to Sophie.

After a brief, awkward hesitation, Sophie held out her own hands and took the girl's with a gentle squeeze. "I'm Gail."

"I haven't met you before," Adele said, pushing her two long braids over her shoulder.

Sophie realized she needed to justify her presence in the barn. "I... just arrived. I'm Marie's niece. I'm staying for a while. Do you live nearby?"

"Next farm over." She pointed back toward the road and then knelt down next to the kittens, scooping one up. She picked up a second one and held the two next to each other. They wriggled in her gentle grasp.

Sophie could hear her heartbeat pounding in her ears and her throat tightened. She clasped her hands in front of her and tried to calm down.

"I can't decide between these two." Adele snuggled the kittens against her chest. "This one," and she bopped it playfully on the nose, "has these adorable mitten feet. And this one," she tickled its neck, "Has the pretty stripes on his tail. See?" She gently pulled his tail straight and let it fall free of her fingers. The kittens rolled around and tried to chase her thumbs. Adele sighed and set them next to their mother, where they immediately tried to squirm their way in for more milk. "But they're all wonderful, don't you think?"

Sophie, who had stopped breathing entirely, assured herself that there was no hidden motive in that question. She forced herself to nod. She blinked. Her eyes were watering and threatening to drip.

The girl got back to her feet, peering up at Sophie. "I'm growing pumpkins this year. I'm going to have the biggest one this fall. Do you like pumpkins? I eat the seeds."

Sophie tore her gaze away from the kittens, trying to breathe normally. "I like pumpkin seeds." Her words sounded flat and desolate to her own ears.

Adele didn't seem to notice and continued, "I'm learning to sew, too. I'm going to make a quilt." Adele lifted her chin proudly.

Sophie tried for more enthusiasm, although she felt like weeping. "I've never sewn before," she said, wondering if sewing was in her approved fictional history. She needed to memorize that better.

Adele grinned. "I could teach you. It's easy. Aunt Marie made the one in her living room. I'm going to make mine with kittens on it instead of flowers, though."

Sophie wondered what she could say that would sound normal. "It sounds beautiful."

"It will be."

Thankfully, before Sophie could mess up her history and the conversation too badly, Raymond arrived. "Ah, there you are, Gail. I wondered if you got lost, but I see you've met our youngest neighbor."

"Hi, Uncle Raymond," Adele said. "I just came to see the kittens."

Raymond rubbed the girl's head affectionately. "They're growing more every day. Just like you."

She giggled.

Raymond grinned and then said, "Maybe this weekend, you and your mom and dad can come have dinner with us, and you can properly meet my niece."

"I'll ask." Adele glanced back at the kittens.

Raymond's eyes twinkled. "Want to help with the chores? I was just headed to the stable to clean out the stalls. It'd be marvelous fun."

Adele wrinkled her nose in mock disgust. "Uh uh. I think I have to go home now. Right now." She skipped off.

Raymond chuckled. "I once teased her that if I was too busy to play with her, I'd ask her to help me with my chores, and ever since then, it's our secret code. She's a good kid." He peered at Sophie, his eyebrows pulling together thoughtfully. "I hope she didn't upset you?"

"I'm fine," Sophie said, too quickly to be reassuring. "I'm sorry I was taking so long."

"No need to apologize. I just thought maybe that fork wasn't where I told you it was, and I came to help look."

"Oh."

He rubbed his chin and then spoke softly, kindly. "We're aware of what was going on at the castle. If you ever want to talk about it..."

"I'm fine," Sophie repeated. "I appreciate the offer though."

As they were collecting the pitchfork, he said, "I'm going to town this afternoon to see if there's any news. Is there anything specific you want me to ask about?"

"Just general news. The things I'm most concerned about would announce my presence here." After a moment, she added, "See if you can find out if the King and Prince are dead?"

"I'll try."

****

"My son told me you were dead, Finn. He called and we sent our military. He's now occupying their capital."

Finn grimaced, taking a seat at the dining room table across from Grayson's father. "Is he ok?" Finn had only just managed to get to the lord's estate. The odd network of people had finally smuggled him to Demense in a crate of very smelly, itchy wool, and then he'd had to beg his own countrymen to take him to a phone. Some of the paranoia had rubbed off on him and he'd refused to discuss anything over an open line. They'd sent an aircar for him immediately.

Lord March answered, "Grayson says he sustained some minor injuries. His doctor tells me he's fighting a vicious infection and that the injuries are not minor. My son will be overjoyed to see you. As I am. What's really going on out there?"

"I probably know less than you. I've spent the last month being shuffled around their country, blindfolded, in trunks and boxes. No one would tell me anything. They barely spoke to me, except to tell me terse directions. The only thing I can say is that apparently the truth was worse than the rumors."

"That's what Grayson says although he wont go into any detail. We're getting some of our people back who are describing horrific things. Impossible things." The old lord tapped his fingers on the table. "Are you willing to go back? Grayson needs a friend out there and I can't go."

"Absolutely. I've been kicking myself for letting us get separated in the first place."

"He said you didn't have any choice."

Finn rolled his head on his shoulders, trying to get the tension-stiff muscles to relax. "Let me get a bath and fresh clothes and a good night's sleep. I'll go tomorrow."

"Do you want to surprise him or do you want me to tell him you're here?"

"Go ahead and tell him. No reason to prolong it," Finn said tiredly. Once upon a lifetime ago, he and Grayson were always surprising each other and playing pranks.

"I'm glad you're alive, Finn. Go keep my son that way."

"Yes, Milord." Finn stood and left the room. He could feel the anxiety he'd been carrying finally releasing. Grayson was ok.

****

Sophie could feel her heart pounding. Wyatt was still alive. He was somewhere in the country, probably viciously destroying people in his anger. Anxiety threatened to paralyze her. Grayson March, a lord of Demense, had come to their rescue and failed.

They were going to lose it all. Wyatt would already be summoning and preparing his army. If he managed to take the throne, no one would recover. She put her head on the table and wept.

Marie came around the kitchen table and put her hand on Sophie's back. "They'll catch him, pet."

"No, they won't," Sophie sobbed. "He's too smart. He's too dangerous. Nothing will bring him out into the open until he's ready to strike and they wont stand a chance. It'll be a massacre."

Raymond said, "He wont be able to hide. Lord March has taken the media networks and has been broadcasting pictures and offering a reward."

"People are too afraid to turn him in." Sophie wiped her eyes on her sleeve. "I have to find him first." She swallowed. She knew what had to be done. "There is one thing that'll lure him out." She inhaled and exhaled, biting her trembling lower lip. "Me. He's always wanted me, but the King stopped him."

"No, pet. You're to stay here, where it's safe," Marie said sternly.

Sophie gazed at Raymond. "You said Lord March controls the media?"

Raymond nodded.

"Is he also broadcasting pictures of me?"

Raymond looked away. "Yes."

"But you look different now," Marie countered. "You're safe here."

"I'll go get publicly arrested. Wyatt'll come for me. He'll risk it before he's ready. I'll have Lord March's army protecting me. It's our only chance. We've got to kill him or no one is safe."

****

Grayson shifted as the doctor carefully wiped at his back. He was seated sideways on the chair in the small room he'd claimed as his office. He'd chosen the smaller space with a huge desk simply because it cut down on the number of people who could badger him at the same time.

"Hold still," the doctor reprimanded.

Grayson continued to fidget happily. Finally, something good had happened - they had her! The idiot had openly walked into one of the news centers, demanded to be interviewed to share her side, and stuck around long enough for his people to arrive and arrest her. The news media was playing the Princess' interview on repeat, but he didn't care about that. The headline 'War Criminal Arrested' was satisfying enough, but his favorite quote from the interview was, "My brother thinks he can unseat our new King. He's delusional and he'll never get what he always wanted."

She'd named Grayson King. He and his advisors had been discussing if and when to do that. His people had already latched onto it and were calling him 'Your Majesty' and forcing the staff and locals to do the same. It was unbelievable luck. If only they could get the Prince to do something equally stupid, but Grayson knew it wouldn't be that easy.

And Finn! Finn was on his way. How had he survived? This was a good day.

****

This was a bad day. Sophie cradled her left arm. It had been broken during her arrest when one of the men had thrown her against the newsroom wall. That was minor. The entire way back to the castle, she kept telling her guards that her brother would come and they needed to be ready. They had ignored her, and then, annoyed that she kept insisting, they covered her mouth with tape. She still tried.

They got to the castle and locked her in one of the arena's cells. The other cells were empty. She managed to get the tape off of her mouth and yelled warnings until she was hoarse. The two guards across the the cell had simply covered their ears, shook their heads at each other, and smirked at her.

She felt at her palms, feeling the wooden lockpicks buried in the muscle by her thumb. They'd been embedded there so long she'd forgotten them. They were part of Pieran's 'how to get out of the dungeon' training. Would they even come out? Could she remember how to pick handcuff locks? She could feel them if she pressed and pushed her finger the right way. She started scraping at the skin of her palms, trying to open a hole. Then she was suddenly afraid of exposing the tip and stopped.

Two guards. Two lousy guards against Wyatt. Maybe she should find a way to kill herself? Death was certainly preferable to her brother's dungeon. She peered around the sparse cell. Anything potentially useful had long since been removed to protect the arena combatants. Sweat, blood, and tears seemed to saturate the rough stone walls.

Sophie went to the sink and drank some water. Maybe she could survive long enough for Lord March to track down Wyatt? Maybe her brother hadn't had time to set up a another dungeon. If it were a rushed build, it would be easier to escape. Her arm hurt. She paced. She tried to warn the guards again. She paced more.

Unfortunately, she didn't have to wait long. She heard quiet popping sounds and saw both guards drop to the floor. Sophie screamed as loudly as she could and then abruptly stopped when Wyatt ambled in, swinging cell keys on his index finger. He had four armed men at his side.

"Oh, my dear sister," he said softly, shaking his head in false amazement. "You know I always get what I want." He kicked one of the dead guards. "I expected more guards in here. True, that imposter had quite a few outside, but I still would have expected more in here. They probably couldn't stand your screeching. I'll have to punish you for that, but not yet."

Sophie, frozen, realized she'd have to stay conscious in order to count the steps and turns to get out of a dungeon maze in the dark. She couldn't afford to provoke him.

Wyatt walked over to the cell door and unlocked it. "Come on, Sophie, don't make me come in there for you."

Sophie looked down, mimicking the wisest of the slaves, and stepped forward until she was out of the cell. She stopped near him.

"That obedience is a start. Now, I want you to come over and kiss me and then look up at the camera and wave. I've cut the sound, but we should leave a video of us departing as friends."

Sophie did as she was told. She even managed a smile at the cold round glass that refused to send help.

****

Pieran lay in his cell, studying the odd cement patterns on the ceiling. The cells in Demense were clean and brightly lit. The mattress, while thin, was comfortable enough and he had a pillow, sheets, and a simple red jumpsuit. The sink and toilet were functional and had drinkable water. They brought three nutritious meals per day and let him walk in a cement courtyard in the sunlight once every other day. The guards were honorable men and while firm, they weren't brutal or cruel. Showers, after the initial commentary on his bruises and scars, were uneventful and came with a clean jumpsuit.

His physical body was healing while he was going mentally crazy, torn between his grief over Blair's death and his desperation for news. What had happened? Were the King and Prince dead? Pieran hadn't gotten a chance to share the passcodes because that pilot had knocked him unconscious. The time for passcodes was long gone by now anyway.

Where was Sophie? If she'd made it to the network, they would have sent her out to that farm by the Gressuf Mountains. It was not only the safest place for her, it was the best location they had in their network. Most people who had any degree of wealth were unwilling to risk it, but that farm was remote enough that Sophie could stay indefinitely.

Pieran asked a passing guard again if he could speak with the local lord. The guard assured him that they had conveyed his request to speak to someone in charge and told him that his lord was simply too busy with other matters and that he'd be heard eventually.

****

Sophie counted steps. She didn't dare look into any of the cells they passed. She should have realized that Wyatt would have dungeons outside of the castle, complete with their modern electronics, traps, and bombs. She had to believe escape would be possible. She certainly wasn't going to be rescued. Wyatt hadn't even bothered to blindfold her, such was his confidence. He'd driven right up to a stonework house and escorted her in as if she were a treasured guest - a securely bound guest, but still, a guest.

The sounds of people crying and moaning that had so terrified her when she was a child were merely background noise to her counting. They didn't bother her; she was too focused. They turned into a cell and Sophie glanced about, searching for potential weapons. She didn't have to feign terror at what she saw.

"Nice, isn't it?" Wyatt said. "It's got all the modern enhancements. I think you know what comes first."

The zombie-eyed guard with them pushed Sophie toward the table and lifted her onto it.

Wyatt walked over to her side. "I let some reports slip out over the years so you'd be prepared and wouldn't be scared of dying."

The guard was securing her feet and arms.

Wyatt's eyes narrowed and he poked her broken arm. "That's wasteful," he commented. "I'll have to punish you for letting yourself get damaged. I know you were using yourself as bait." He took her arm with both of his hands and pulled the bones apart and let them fall back into their rightful place.

Sophie screamed.

****

It was lightless, not dark, but completely lightless. She could hear the sobbing and cries of the others. She was damaged and she had agony in places that shouldn't be possible to hurt. She needed to escape now. She'd only get more injured over time. There would be no recovery.

After saying that he was leaving for dinner, Wyatt had left her on the cold metal table, handcuffed so she could be easily moved later to the more permanent manacles when he was done playing and was ready to keep her as a trophy. Her feet were cuffed and pulled upwards at a right angle to her body, 'to keep your intestines from falling out', Wyatt had said, even though he'd stitched the gash closed again. She'd deal with that when she got to it. One thing at a time.

First her palms. She scratched at the tops of the lockpicks on both hands. They became slick with blood, but eventually she found the tops. The wooden stick on her left hand, the side with the broken arm, snapped as she pulled it free, rendering it useless. She needed to be more careful with the angle as she extracted the other one. It came free, tugging painfully at the attached flesh, and she nearly dropped it. Hoping it would be sturdy enough, she carefully and gently slid it into the handcuff. She took a deep breath and pushed.

The handcuff fell open, but she dropped the pick. Sophie felt around on the table until she found it and reached across and undid the other side. The leg rigging was secured to the side of the table so Wyatt could easily adjust it. She reached for it, screaming as her midriff tried to tear open. She untied the rope and her feet fell to the table with a thud.

Where had she left the pick? No, they weren't locks. They were buckles. If Sophie could get her hands to her ankles, she could undo them. She reached down to her right thigh and hauled it up, shrieking with the pain and effort. At least Wyatt's dungeons were soundproof. She didn't have to worry about anyone other than the other prisoners hearing her and they had to be used to her screams by now. She got the buckle open.

Sophie's broken left arm wouldn't be able to lift her left thigh. She'd have to sit up. She groaned and told herself that at least she'd find out if her innards were going to spill out. She grabbed the side of the table and yanked on it, rolling slightly to her side and then using her elbow to push herself up. She felt blood dripping down her stomach and used her left hand to hold the wound closed.

Someone else decided to scream along with her, either in sympathy or boredom. Maybe in sheer animal connection. By the time Sophie had the other ankle undone, she had a symphony of equally anguished voices joining hers.

She slid off of the table, holding her abdomen with her broken arm. If she could find the tape, she could use that to hold herself together. She closed her eyes, even though she didn't need to, and tried to see where Wyatt had put it. She worked her way over to the small table and found the tape. She ran it around her wrist and up over her good shoulder and then down between her legs. She couldn't get it around her back so she would have to make do. She secured her arm across the gash on her belly as well as she could. She used the entire roll of tape. She located the scalpel, her chosen weapon, and found the cell door. No need for locked doors in here. Prisoners weren't going anywhere and Wyatt didn't like the delays of locks beyond the first one.

Sophie reversed the counting. Clutching the scalpel tightly, she hobbled. She bounced into a wall at the first turn and realized her steps were smaller. She adjusted her count and hoped she wouldn't get lost. She counted and turned and ignored the sobbing and wails.

Her toe smacked into the bottom stair. She'd made it. She climbed to the top stair. Now she just needed to wait, without passing out, for Wyatt to open the door. Sophie remembered that the door opened outward. Wyatt would open it before he turned on the master light switch. He'd want to revel in the cries of terror that the light coming on would bring. That was how he announced his arrival.

Sophie had seen the light switch on her way in, seen him turn it on. Heard the keening resonance. She remembered where he stood, how far he opened the door, where his zombie guard waited deferentially out of the way. It didn't matter about the guard. If she could kill Wyatt, she won whether or not the guard killed her. She wouldn't worry about him. She would focus entirely on Wyatt. His leg would be there and she could reach that. He wouldn't have armor on. He didn't need armor. He was invincible. He had guards and subservient slaves. She saw every step in her mind. She kept moving and stretching her legs and good arm to make sure they wouldn't stiffen.

When the door beeped and swung open, Sophie was ready. She launched herself upwards, first slicing his thigh, then up his hip, and into his arm that swung down to stop her. She ran the blade up and over and into the side of his neck, ripping the blade back and forth across the thick vein there.

Wyatt grabbed her broken arm and pulled as he dropped to the floor, gurgling. Sophie's shriek was echoed by the occupants below.

The guard grasped at Sophie's hair, but it was too short for him to get a good grip and she swung the blade up and into the center of his stomach, twisting and grinding it upwards. He grunted and swung a fist, cracking her in the side of her head. She let go of the scalpel and twisted around behind the guard and shoved him down the stairs. She wanted to slam the door shut, but if she did, every person down there would die, because she didn't have the passcode to open it again.

Instead, she flipped the light on and looked in. The sound the occupants made at that light resonated through her body and the keening wails burned into her soul. The guard had landed on the scalpel and wasn't moving. Wyatt reached weakly toward her ankle. She bent down and dug her fingers into the hole at his neck and tore it wider. Blood sprayed rather than seeping. She ripped at it, shredding his throat until the blood stopped flowing, and he stopped twitching.

Sophie glanced again at the unmoving guard and went in search of a knife. She found one in a quaint, bright orange kitchen and went back. She started with the guard, cutting his neck until she was sure he wouldn't rise and then she went back to Wyatt. She ran the blade into his eye socket and scrambled his brain. She didn't want some demented medical experiment able to resurrect him.

Sophie stared at the body. It wasn't enough. She cut open his pants and sliced that off too. She became aware that she was shivering. She needed a phone before the adrenalin wore off. Hadn't she seen one in the kitchen? She dropped the knife and went back.

She found an envelope on the counter and hoped that was the right address. It took three tries for her to get the pickup number right. Her voice was barely audible as she answered the questions. Sophie only had to survive another 30 minutes and then they'd be there for her with a doctor. The original estimate was 45 minutes until they'd learned that she was critically injured. She knew she ought to go down into the dungeon and free the occupants, but she couldn't make herself do it. She could still hear the sound of the light and the anguish she'd caused by turning it on.

She waited 25 minutes and then called the nearest hospital. "Help me, please. I've fallen down our basement stairs. There's no one home and I can't get up." She gave them the address. "I can't remember if I locked the front door or not. You might have to smash the window to get in. I broke my leg for sure and I may have fractured my hip. I hope I haven't broken my back. Please hurry! Owwww! Oh no! My battery's dying." She swore and hung up.

It had been 30 minutes. Bracing herself for the pain, she pushed herself up and stumbled to the front door. The aircar was already there and two men were approaching. They saw her and ran forward, catching her as she fell.

****

Grayson leaned forward, his elbows on the desk, with his face in his hands. He'd lost 34 good men when the Prince had come to rescue his sister. They'd taunted him, smiling and waving into the security camera, before strolling out as if they were taking a walk in a park.

Grayson wasn't going to arrest her. He was going to kill her. Same for her brother. He'd deal with the international repercussions of that later.

How had the Prince gotten such a large army so fast? He could have sworn they were scattered and disorganized. They had shown up and walked through his defenses like they weren't even there. Conveniently, the security footage leading up to the attack and through the attack were missing. The only video that remained was the soundless clip of the Prince collecting the Princess from her cell and the two of them waving and walking out hand-in-hand.

The extra troops from Demense had arrived two days too late to be of help. They even sent some computer techs and found that the Prince had been in the surveillance network watching them the entire time despite the system changes. It made him queasy. At least that was now shut down.

Grayson stretched and winced as his back complained. That annoying doctor would be around soon to change his bandages again.

The door opened and Finn peered in. "So, how's your day going, Your Majesty?"

Grayson groaned. "Ugh."

Finn entered and closed the door. "Yeah, well, you're gonna love this. I just got a report from some backwards town called Brennan's Creek. It's west of here." He sat down opposite Grayson. "I've already sent out a unit. They found another dungeon."

"What?" Grayson's head snapped up alertly.

"Open. And you'll never guess who was laying in a pool of his own blood, chopped to pieces, at the entrance. They think it's the Prince. They're saying one of the prisoners escaped and killed him. There's apparently a significant blood trail back to one of the cells."

"No," Grayson said with disbelief.

Finn nodded. "Oh yes. The hospital got a call saying someone got hurt so they sent an ambulance. The hospital's going to be overrun. They're already calling for backup. They need a fleet of surgeons and operating rooms. It's a nightmare."

"I hate this country."

"Well, King, too bad; it's your country now. I'm going out to oversee the rescue operations. They're going to need someone who can speak for you and I can identify the Prince's body and tell you if it's really him."

Grayson shook his head. "You don't want to see it. I've been through dungeons that were mostly destroyed. Trust me. Leave it to the others."

"The people that got me out of the country said if they hadn't, I would have been taken to one. I need to see it."

Grayson frowned. "That's an order from your King. You're to stay here."

"You don't want to be King of this country anyway. I'll bring you a report." Finn got up and left with a partial salute.

Chapter 4

Sophie whimpered.

"Shhh. We got you. You're safe now."

A hand pressed a cool cloth to her forehead. It felt good.

"I don't know what to do with this." The woman's unfamiliar voice sounded panicked.

"Get the castle doctor. His name's Oscar. He's got experience." That voice was familiar, but Sophie couldn't place it.

Another voice that she didn't recognize, said, "He's out at Brennan's Creek. He's not going to be able to come."

"We could take her out there."

"No, the place is crawling with Lord March's army."

"You're going to have to do your best, Doctor."

"We have to cut her open and make sure he didn't put anything inside before we run scans. Any metal will kill her."

"Give her something to put her to sleep first."

"Can't without a blood test. If we mix the wrong drugs, that would kill her too. We don't know what he gave her. I need a real hospital. Not this."

"You're going to need another blood donor too. I'm starting to feel lightheaded."

Darkness swirled around Sophie. She thought, 'Leave the lights on. It's not the dark I'm afraid of; it's the sound the light makes when it comes on.'

****

Pieran knew by the language and accents when his fellow countrymen started joining him in the prison. They were angry, indignant, and complained loudly, demanding to be let free, shouting that the marauder should withdraw. They insisted that the country be given back to the Queen.

Sophie was probably still alive! Pieran could have danced. He celebrated by going over to the sink and washing his face. He returned to his bed and lay there enjoying the hope.

After several nights of listening to them rant, however, he couldn't stop himself from thinking that in order to shut them up, the guards only needed to crack one of them on the side of the head and threaten to send them to a dungeon. Pieran hated himself for the thought. He rolled away from the bars and pulled the pillow over his head to try to find the peaceful quiet again.

Over the next month, more of his countrymen continued to arrive in waves. They were mostly farmers. Local prisoners were transferred to make room and Pieran was moved from his private cell into the general population. He was finally able to make discreet inquiries. None of his countrymen had actually seen Sophie. The Prince was rumored to be dead. The Wallace Lords, out on the edges of the country, were warring against Lord March, who had declared himself King. While the Wallace Lords had weapons because Pieran had directed them to discreetly stockpile for the last decade, the farmers weren't trained in actual use of those weapons. People on both sides were dying needlessly.

Pieran didn't tell the men who he was. He knew they would rally around him and demand leadership and there wasn't much he could do from inside the prison. Thankfully, security had prevented his real name from ever being used outside of Central.

Where was Sophie? They'd talked about this possibility. Their country needed to be put back together as quickly as possible. Revolutions were bloody affairs. It didn't matter whether she took over or if the new government did, but they didn't want an extended war. The people had been hurt for too long.

****

Sophie ran her fingers over the large bandage across her abdomen, feeling the contours of the thick packing material there. The pain was bearable, but only because she knew Wyatt was finally dead. He couldn't hurt anyone anymore.

When she lifted her good arm to inspect the healing cuts there, the woman sitting beside her stirred. The woman said, "Can I get you anything, Your Majesty? Some water, maybe? Juice?"

Sophie inhaled. Using her voice still hurt. "Do you have a name? Or... have you told me already?"

"Just call me 'medtech', Your Majesty. We're still maintaining security." The medtech reached over and flipped a switch and the room's dim light brightened. Sophie was in one of the small houses in Risell somewhere, occupying someone's main bedroom.

"Why? The King and Prince are dead."

"I don't know, Your Majesty. Habit, I suppose."

"Could you find Madame Violet for me?" They'd already told her Pieran was somewhere in their new King's prison system. With Blair dead, Madame Violet would be the next in line, inasmuch as they had a line.

"You mean Jo? I think she's here somewhere. I'll go get her."

The medtech left.

Sophie again lifted her arm and looked at it. She'd have some decorative scarring if her abdomen wound didn't kill her. She let her arm fall back down.

The door opened slightly. "Your Majesty?" Noah stuck his head in.

"Come in, Noah. Please."

The boy hesitantly stepped in and quickly closed the door. "I'm not supposed to disturb you, but I thought maybe..." His hands twisted together uncomfortably.

"What's wrong?"

"I'm sorry I let you down."

"What? What do you mean?"

"I gave them the list. I don't know why they didn't use it. I found someone that had a lot of bars and stripes on his uniform, but I must have picked the wrong person. I'm sorry. I got them killed."

"No, Noah, you didn't. You tried to save them. We all tried to save them. You taking those passcodes was the bravest, noblest thing I've ever seen. Don't you ever apologize for that."

"But, Your Majesty, they died. I failed."

"You didn't fail. It was always unlikely we'd be able to save them. Please stop calling me 'Your Majesty'. Isn't... Um. what was his name? Lord..."

"Lord March."

"Yeah, him. Lord March. Isn't he King?"

"He says he is, but you're the Queen now."

"Is he a good King, Noah?"

"He doesn't hurt anyone. Well, not unless they attack him. There's fighting out by the Wallace Lords. Lord March has open courts and says anyone can come in with a petition."

"Does he..." Sophie murmured. "I wonder. Pieran's still under arrest, right?"

"Yes, Your Majesty."

"Want to do something else brave for me?"

"Anything, Your Majesty."

"Stop calling me 'Your Majesty', please. Use 'Milady' if you have to use a title. I need someone to go to our new King and ask for Pieran's release. Be respectful. Treat him like he's our real King, because he is. Call him 'Your Majesty'."

"But you're our Queen."

"No, Noah. Not anymore. I'm too tired, too broken. Even if I wanted to be, which I don't, I can't possibly rule our kingdom. I'm physically not able to. We need to give Lord March our full support. We need to keep our country from tearing itself apart. People are dying in those fights by the Wallace Lords. You understand? We have to save them now."

Noah appeared to think this over. "Are you sure you don't want to be Queen? Everyone will support you."

"I'm more sure of that than I've been of anything in my entire life, Noah. If he's a good King, we need to keep him." One of the worst things the new King could do right now would be to pack up and leave their country in chaos. She might die yet anyway.

Noah straightened and lifted his shoulders. "What do you want me to say, Milady?"

****

From the throne, Grayson studied the courtiers. How many of them were plotting his death? The computer techs had managed to recover some of the deleted security video from the Princess' rescue. Servants had spread word amongst each other and had joined forces with the Prince's men to overtake his own people. It was the craziest thing. A whisper, a sudden paling, a pained look, and a nod. Followed by treachery and murder.

A boy entered the room. He was perhaps in his mid-teens, which was odd. The country seemed to be missing people between the ages of 7 and 35. Then again, maybe it wasn't odd. They were probably hiding. That was demographic of the dead in the dungeons. The kid looked terrified. His eyes passed over the room and locked onto Grayson.

Grayson waved him forward and the kid hesitated a moment and then stepped up to the edge of the carpet in front of the throne.

The kid kneeled and bowed his head, looking studiously at the carpet. He swallowed. "Your Majesty, I'm here to request the release of the slave named Pieran. He was mistakenly arrested when your people arrived in our country. He is an old man and hasn't done anything against you."

Grayson's eyes narrowed. None of the locals called him by his new position without prompting from his own men. Which of his people felt they needed to send this boy instead of asking him directly? Was the insanity of these people spreading to his own people? Grayson cleared his throat. "Pieran helped a war criminal escape. He's imprisoned for that. There will be a trial eventually and we'll determine his innocence then."

The kid winced, nodded, and replied, "Thank you for hearing my request, Your Majesty." He got to his feet, bowed, and retreated.

Grayson leaned over to Finn and whispered, "Find out who that was."

"On it." Finn left through the door behind the throne.

Grayson sighed. He needed to spend more time among his troops, encouraging them to talk to him. If they'd've just come to him directly and said, 'Hey, you should release that poor abused slave; he probably didn't have any choice.', he could have quietly let the man go. He probably should have done so before now, anyway. Now he had to publicly justify his decision.

He'd just been so incredibly busy. Even with the added troops, he didn't have enough men. Across the country, there were deadly attacks on key infrastructure points and his sparse outposts. He had people looking in nearby towns for more dungeons. They'd found another, but it had destroyed itself and killed 2 of his own people when they tried to get in. He had agents spread out around the country searching for that Princess, too.

As if that weren't enough, he had to constantly defend and control the news media. One day, they'd be airing the truth, that people had been tortured and killed in dungeons and that their new King was trying to restore order. Then, the next day, the same station would tell people to follow this or that man and behead the intruder and restore the rightful Queen of the country. The reporters at the stations couldn't be blamed. They said whatever the person pointing the gun at them told them to.

****

Sophie stared at Madame Violet and repeated, "I have to tell the Wallace Lords to stand down. They won't come here. I have to go to them."

"Milady, you can barely stand up."

At least she'd finally convinced Madame Violet to support their new King. If it was that hard to convince someone who knew the facts, how hard was it going to be to convince the Wallace Lords? "The harvest is coming and the farmers are getting arrested and carried away. How many people will starve when there's no food this winter? The Wallace Lords are fools."

"They're supporting you, Milady."

"They shouldn't. The King's accusations aren't wrong. I've done horrible things."

"You're as much a victim as any of those our King is now protecting."

"You will stay here and keep trying to stop the attacks on the media buildings. Noah can come with me."

"Noah's just a boy. I don't know what you think he'll be able to do."

Sophie closed her eyes. Noah would be her friend and would do it without arguing everything. She was so incredibly drained and she had so much to do. "Have him come talk with me. I'll see if he wants to."

"Yes, Milady." Madame Violet adjusted Sophie's blanket and left.

Sophie had no doubt that the woman would tell her son to politely decline, but Sophie really needed someone by her side that she could completely trust to not do things 'for her own good'. If that person was too young, so be it. She wasn't that much older herself.

When Noah arrived, he was still a boy. Sophie told him what she needed. She told him what she'd done and why the King thought she was a war criminal, in explicit detail. She explained her medical situation. She predicted the potential consequences, both the good and bad, and discussed the alternatives. If she died, the rebellion wouldn't have any choice but to declare defeat and fall in behind their new King. She named other possibilities that would put their country back together, too. When Noah left, he was a man. He would accompany her.

****

Noah listened to the gruff older men talking over Sophie. It was infuriating. They were demanding she take her place as the rightful Queen while completely ignoring her. This was their third stop and the other two had gone the same.

They discussed battle tactics and logistics and now that they knew for certain she was alive, they were reinvigorated in their need for a swift victory. Every time she tried to say something, they told her that they were wiser and more experienced in these matters and that she needed to let them handle it. She could concern herself with matters of the court once she was on the throne, but now was a time for war and the removal of the invader.

Noah studied Sophie, seeing the beads of sweat at her hairline and the tremble in her hand as she tried to speak again. The pain medicine she'd taken just before the meeting was wearing off. The bench in the barn wasn't comfortable for him and he didn't have her wounds. He took her cup from the makeshift slat table and went over to the hose and refilled it. He brought it back and set it on the table, discreetly leaving another pill on the table next to it.

Sophie palmed the medicine and unobtrusively swallowed it with some of the water. Noah thought that if she were healthier, she could have yelled at them, maybe could have forced her way into their conversation. Noah tried not to be angry at them; Sophie had directed him not to be. They were loyal men and they had taken in many refugees over the years, himself included. They knew what the King had been and what the Prince had been and were glad to be rid of them. They also knew that Sophie had been leading the network and saving whomever she could. They just wouldn't acknowledge that Sophie not only didn't want to be their Queen but that she wasn't physically up to the task.

After more of this, Sophie reached over and touched Noah's shoulder. Noah nodded at the signal and helped her stand.

The men also stood.

"I appreciate your loyalty," Sophie said, "But I need to go now. I can't stay in one place very long or I'll be discovered."

Their leader bowed, "Of course, Your Majesty. We understand. While we're happy to see you, you shouldn't put yourself at risk like this. We'll manage and we'll have you back in the castle soon. I promise."

Noah helped Sophie to the door and once they were out of sight, he picked her up and carried her back to the aircar. She wasn't that heavy. He arranged her on the thick pillows in the back seat. He was as gentle as he could be, but he knew he scared her when he leaned over her at certain angles.

As they flew back toward the network house they would stay at that evening, Sophie murmured, "This isn't going to work, Noah."

"No, Milady, it isn't."

"We'll head back to Central tomorrow."

Noah glanced into the rearview mirror and saw that she was crying.

****

Grayson picked at his dinner, not really hungry. The meat and vegetable stew was exquisitely prepared; the old King liked his food and had kept a good kitchen staff. At least he was able to eat in his private office tonight. He despised the necessary dinners with the courtiers. Those affairs needed guards and food tasters and the courtiers watched him, mimicking him, trying to avoid upsetting him. He was incredibly tired of people being afraid of him, but they'd lived in fear so long that it was their ingrained survival mechanism.

He wanted to go home. When he'd come to this country, it was for a simple reconnaissance, not a permanent relocation. Other, more experienced people were supposed to take over for the actual invasion if it was deemed necessary. He pushed a piece of cauliflower to the side in search of another chunk of meat.

The door opened and Finn entered without knocking.

Grayson rubbed his temple. "What is it this time?"

"You remember that kid I couldn't find? The one that disappeared like salt in water?"

"Yeah?"

"He's back. He says he has a question for you."

"What is it?"

"He wouldn't tell me."

Grayson sighed. "Bring him in."

Finn reached across the desk and took one of the rolls. He gave another of his teasing salutes and departed.

Grayson muttered, "Now what?" and pushed his dish to the side.

A short time later, Finn brought the boy in.

The kid saw Grayson, dropped to his knees, looking at the floor, and said, "Your Majesty, thank you for seeing me."

Behind the kid, Finn shrugged and shook his head.

Grayson frowned. "Stand up."

The kid climbed to his feet. "Yes, Your Majesty." He still kept his gaze downcast.

"I understand you have a question for me?" Grayson noticed his own finger tapping unconsciously and stilled it. Such an action might indicate impatience or anger. He hated having to be aware of every movement and having to carefully censor every word he spoke.

"Yes, Your Majesty." The boy inhaled, shaking slightly. "Milady, Sophie Renault, would like to meet with you. Will you accept the meeting?"

Grayson blinked. As neutrally and calmly as he could, he asked, "Where is she?"

"I don't know, Your Majesty. She'll have moved from where I last saw her."

Grayson gripped the edge of the desk. He would not leap across and throttle the kid, but he wanted to. The boy would have been tortured and twisted into compliance or he was being blackmailed. Had he been serving her when he asked for Pieran's release? That poor kid. If he said no, what repercussions would the kid suffer? No wonder he was shaking.

Grayson nodded, but the kid was still adamantly staring at the floor. "I'll accept the meeting," he said.

Behind the boy, Finn raised an eyebrow.

The kid reached into his shirt and withdrew a white envelope. He set it on the table and waited. His shoulders were tense and he swallowed again.

"Finn," Grayson said, "Show our young messenger out of the castle and come back here. See that no one impedes him."

"Um. Ok." Finn's quizzical gaze would have to wait. He added after a second's delay, "Yes, Your Majesty."

Finn tapped the boy on the shoulder and the kid bowed, saying almost inaudibly, "Thank you, Your Majesty."

As soon as the door shut, Grayson reached across the desk and snatched the envelope. The handwritten letter simply said, "Sire, I will meet you tomorrow at noon at the courtyard table in Risell where I ate my lunch. I have arranged an escort to prevent misunderstandings. - Sophie"

****

The appalling dread Sophie felt was almost equal to the the physical pain that was trying to kill her. She planned to wait until the very last minute to take one of the stronger pain pills.

She extended her arm and let Madam Violet pull the long sleeve on. The dress material was as light as the seamstress could make it and still have it opaque. Both sleeves, as well as the waistline of her underwear had pain pills sewn in. They'd replaced the heavier cast on her arm with a much lighter weight clear plastic that might help her maneuver more freely. They had also tried a supportive corset, but even loosely bound, it still caused too much pain. The bandages would have to do.

Noah reached around and held the dress material so it wouldn't pull on her as Madame Violet adjusted it. "The dress opens here, Milady," he said. "You'll be able to use the bathroom without lifting the material."

"You'll remember to ask about the harvest?" Sophie said.

"I will," he answered. "I wish I could think of a different way than this."

"Me, too," Madam Violet grumbled. She wasn't happy, but she'd been overruled. "It's going to get you killed." She finished tying the front of the dress closed.

The front buttons and ribbons ensured that Sophie should be able to get out of the dress by herself if she needed to. They'd chosen a soft pink with faint white florals in an effort to make her seem more delicate and vulnerable.

Noah shook his head. "He's not going to hurt me, Mom. If he wanted to, he would have last night."

"What time is it?" Sophie asked. She was really starting to feel sick. She had forced herself to eat breakfast because she didn't know when the next meal might come, but she regretted it.

"You have about 15 minutes," Madame Violet said.

"It's time to go then. Noah, get some water."

"Yes, Milady." He skirted around past them and returned with a full glass. He handed her the two pills and the glass.

Sophie sipped at the water and took the pills, drinking just enough to get the pills to go down. She handed the still full glass back to Noah, who just set it on the floor out of the way. They went down the short hallway to a ladder, which Noah carried her up.

Sophie peeked out of Madam Violet's window. As planned, the courtyard was filled with young children moving about. They were dressed in light pastels and each carried a white or pink flower.

Across the courtyard, their King stood next to the table, his arms crossed unhappily. The man she'd had rescued from the furnace pit was with him. Black clad guards and militia enclosed the courtyard at its perimeter.

"Noah," Sophie breathed. Her voice was barely audible.

"Yes, Milady?"

"Thank you." Sophie let go of the bolt of fabric she'd been unconsciously clutching and took Noah's hand.

Madame Violet opened her shop door and Noah led Sophie out into the cool fall sunlight.

The nearest children saw her and swarmed around her, waving their flowers in the air. The living floral arrangement made its way across the courtyard. When they got close enough that Sophie wouldn't have to shout to be heard, she said, "This is good enough, children."

The children stayed near, but moved to make an opening to the King. One of the youngest girls stepped in front of Sophie and said, "A flower for you." She held up a white flower.

Sophie took it and replied, "Thank you. I'll wear it here." She tucked it into one of the ribbons on the front of her dress.

The little girl smiled proudly and moved to the side with the others.

"This is obscene," the King said. "You realize I'm still going to arrest you whether they're here to witness it or not."

Sophie attempted to speak, but couldn't. She cleared her throat and tried again. "I was hoping you might listen to me first, Sire."

The King gestured abruptly. "Get on with it then."

Sophie closed her eyes briefly, thankful for Noah's presence, and then opened them again and said, "Sire, the Wallace Lords actively oppose you as King and seek to put me on the throne as Queen." She waited and when he didn't speak, she pressed onward before she could lose her nerve. "I propose we end this dispute by getting married."

The King make a choking sound.

Sophie added, "Everyone gets what they want." Except her. Sophie would rather die than take up residence in the castle again. She stayed outwardly calm, though. She had years of experience hiding her true emotions.

"You're a monster and a criminal. I won't go into detail in front of these children, but you and I both know what you do. I won't do a disservice to the parents of these babies by letting you go free."

Sophie bit her lip. "Then I offer myself in exchange for Pieran. Take me. Release him. You saw..." She was having a hard time breathing. "What I put him through. Let him go."

The King shook his head. "This isn't a negotiation. The only place you're going is to my dungeon."

Sophie stiffened as if slapped. Time stopped. Her chest seemed to rip in two. She could hear the sound of light being turned on.

"Milady?" Noah touched her arm and prodded, "Milady?"

She blinked. He probably meant prison, not dungeon. Roughly, she said, "Go home, children."

They dropped their flowers and scattered, dodging between the guards and military, running down the streets to disappear into houses. In the span of a few heartbeats, only Sophie, Noah, the King, and his men remained in the courtyard.

The King gestured and several of his men came up and grabbed Sophie's arms. The King pointed at Noah. "Arrest him too. Assisting a war criminal."

Sophie saw men approach and seize Noah. One of her guards shoved her to get her moving and she lost her balance and fell. The plastic didn't prevent her arm from breaking again as she landed on it. Her forehead hit the cobblestone. She heard Noah yell, "Don't hurt her!"

They dragged her up, commanded her to walk, and when she couldn't, they half-carried her, letting her feet bounce along the cobblestone.

Chapter 5

Sophie couldn't move. The pain pills were mere inches from her face, stitched into her sleeve, and she might as well have not had them. Not even her fingers would obey her.

If they had only thrown her into the arena's cell, she might have been ok. But no, they'd turned off the security cameras, and three of them had taken turns kicking her, extracting justice on behalf of the dungeon victims, telling her what they'd seen for each kick. She tried to protect her abdomen at the expense of her arms and back. Then one of them had stomped on her hip and the loud crack could be heard by all four of them. They'd stopped then and transferred her from the floor to the cot. They pulled the heavy sheet over her and made her look like she was simply resting. Then they'd left.

Sophie didn't start to feel it immediately on account of the two additional pain pills she'd secretly swallowed on the way to the castle. She wasn't afraid of Wyatt coming for her anymore.

****

By lucky chance, Pieran happened to be in the prison courtyard when Noah was brought in. What was he doing here? Was Jo also arrested? Had the network fallen?

They wouldn't put a child into the general population. Pieran went over to one of the guards watching over the courtyard. He pointed at Noah. "That's the son of one of my dearest friends. Do you think you could arrange for me to see him?"

The guard sighed. "He probably got picked up as part of one of the attacks."

Like the rest of his countrymen here, Pieran thought sourly.

"Please," Pieran begged. "I've never caused you any trouble. It's a small thing. He'll be scared. I owe it to his mother."

The guard frowned and said, "I'll see what I can do."

"Thank you!" Pieran shuffled off. He spent the remainder of his time outside, watching for other arrivals, but there were none. Listening to his countrymen complain over dinner was even more insufferable than usual. When he got back to his cell, he paced for a short time and then lay down.

"Come on." The guard appeared by Pieran's cell door.

Pieran hopped up and went along with the guard.

They arrived at another cell. This one had a solid door with a small window, not an open bar cell. The guard said, "I can give you fifteen minutes, no more. Keep your voices down."

Pieran nodded enthusiastically.

The guard let Pieran into the cell and closed the door.

"Pieran!" Noah's voice was too loud.

Pieran held his finger up. He whispered, "We have to speak softly and we only have a few minutes. What's going on?"

"Milady sent me to find you. The Wallace Lords are waging war against the King."

"I know. Is the King dead? Is the Prince? Where is Sophie?"

"The King and Prince are both dead. Milady's been arrested."

Pieran sat down on Noah's bed, his shoulders shaking with relief. She was alive. "Are you certain the Prince is dead? People here are saying that's just a rumor."

Noah glanced toward the door, where the guard might still be able to hear their whispers. "Milady confirms it." He sat next to Pieran on the bed.

"Your mother?"

"I don't know. I didn't see what happened after our arrest."

"I'm sorry, Noah."

"Milady says to tell you she's all right." Noah added, silently mouthing, "She was with the Prince for 12 hours."

Pieran hugged himself, rocking. At least she was talking. Maybe he hadn't taken her into one of his dungeons?

Noah continued, whispering again, "The King arrested her when she went to exchange herself for you."

"She what?" Pieran gasped. That was suicidal. He'd lost her. A trial for her crimes would result in her execution.

"After she offered to marry him to end the argument."

Pieran shook his head and looked up at the ceiling, thinking. She was trying to put the country back together. Not lost yet. Why hadn't she gone directly to the Wallace Lords?

"Milady requests you increase your efforts to get the King to release you."

Pieran nodded.

They sat in silence for a minute and then Noah inquired shakily, "Is it bad in here?"

Pieran remembered he was speaking with a young boy who was probably terrified. "No, it's not bad at all. The guards are mostly nice. Do what they tell you and follow the rules. They won't hurt you."

Noah looked faintly relieved.

"What are you here for anyway, Noah?"

Noah snorted. "Same thing as you. Assisting a war criminal."

"Ah, is that why I'm here? I wondered."

The door opened and the guard gestured for Pieran.

Pieran put his hand on Noah's shoulder and said, "Don't be afraid. You'll be ok."

As the guard escorted Pieran back to his own cell, the man commented, "Friend of the family, huh?"

He'd definitely been able to hear them. Pieran replied, "It's a complex friendship. That's the first trustworthy news I've gotten since I've been here."

"I hadn't heard about the proposal. You think that's true?"

"Noah said it. He has no reason to lie."

"Why does that monster want you out so badly?"

"Guilt, I expect. Probably trying to make up for abusing me all those years." Pieran, however, had many reasons to lie.

****

Grayson sat behind his desk on which several stacks of books and papers were strewn about. A half-full mug of beer leaned precariously on a pile of papers to the side. He looked up as the door opened.

The guards released Noah's arms and stepped back.

"What do you need from me, Sire?" Noah asked. He crossed his arms in front of him and his chains' rattled flatly in the small chamber, sound absorbed by the thick tapestries on the walls. He seemed older and less intimidated than he'd been on his other audiences.

"The Princess is dead." Grayson watched Noah's reaction carefully.

Noah's Adams apple bounced as he swallowed. "Did she die here?"

"No. When we discovered she was injured, we took her to the hospital where a group of people, presumably your countrymen, interrupted the transfer before any medical care could be given. She was abducted by them."

Noah's eyes closed a moment and he inhaled deeply. "Did you see her body?"

"You knew she was injured?" Grayson squinted at the boy in surprise.

"I did, Sire. If she had wanted you to know, she would have said something. Did you see her body?" Noah repeated. His voice held a harsh, desperate edge.

"No. The announcement is apparently from a verified, trusted news source and has been not been contradicted."

Noah exhaled and his tension released. He chewed on his lip and then said, "She's not dead. It's a ruse to give her some peace while she's recovering."

Grayson leaned forward. "What hold does she have on you, Noah?"

Noah blinked in confusion. "Sire?"

"What did she threaten you with? One of your family members? A friend? I can protect you. I can take care of it."

Noah's eyes narrowed. His hand unconsciously stroked his lower lip. "Sire, I do not want," and he emphasized the word with a sneer,

"Protection offered by someone who can kill a man's wife in front of him, and then lock that man away in a cell, forgetting him. I'm told you witnessed some of the torture Pieran endured. Why are you punishing him?"

"I am not the monster here!" Grayson barked. They should be praising him for dethroning those psychopaths, not fighting him every step of the way.

Noah stiffened and he paled, but he replied sharply, "You aren't Pieran's personal hero right now either." After a touch of insulting delay, he added, "Sire."

"He helped a war criminal escape. She was dangerous and if she's still alive, she could be hurting some innocent right now. Do you want that? Where would she go?"

"Sire, even if I knew, I wouldn't tell you."

"Like you didn't say anything during that whole absurd conversation in the courtyard? Are you that scared of her?"

"As I recall, I shouted for you not to hurt her as you watched your men throw her to the ground and smash her face into the cobblestone. Sire."

"Noah, I'm going to get you psychiatric counseling. You've been brainwashed. I'm dropping the charges against you as I don't believe you had a choice helping her. If you want to tell me anything that can help someone you love, just let the doctor know and I'll take care of it." Grayson nodded at the two guards.

As the guards stepped forward and grabbed Noah's upper arms, Noah asked, "What about Pieran, Sire? Will you continue to keep him in a locked cell? What are you doing about the harvest?"

Grayson watched as Noah was pulled from the room. Such pride and righteousness in that young man and he obviously didn't believe the Princess was dead. The door closed and the silence returned. Grayson pushed at the stack of papers, clearing a space in front of him and put his arms and head down on the desk. He felt like weeping. Why did he feel like he was defeated?

Noah didn't act scared. He didn't appear to be blackmailed. He didn't even seem like he was tortured to craziness. Yet Grayson had seen it for himself, no, experienced it. He knew what she was capable of.

His head hurt. He was going to have to keep trying to find the Princess and as she was likely dead, it was just a waste of his already limited manpower. And that comment about the harvest! The depth of understanding in that question suggested Noah was playing him, pushing him, or being controlled by someone who was. The problems with the harvest were only just becoming apparent.

Grayson swore. Most of the country's able men were in his prisons for continuing the war against his invasion. There were simply not enough people to bring in the crops. He'd already received reports that entire fields were being lost. This was an agricultural country. It needed that food to survive the upcoming winter. What was Noah's part in this?

Grayson summoned Finn.

"I want full time surveillance on Noah and Pieran. Noah is on his way to Clyde's Psychiatric Hospital. Get that set up and then I want Pieran released and you to follow him and personally handle the surveillance. I want to know every person they talk with and what they say."

"But the royal family is dead. What's the point?" Finn came over to the desk, callously pushed a bunch of old harvest ledgers to the side, and sat on the desk.

"Noah thinks the Princess is still alive. He's terrified of her. Won't tell me what she's coercing him with."

Finn nodded. "Have you read the report from the doctor? She said the Princess was covered in bruises indicative of internal bleeding from getting beaten, but she was already bandaged. I went to talk with the doctor but she's taken a leave of absence. Her supervisor said she didn't give a return date." Finn shrugged. "The people certainly think the Princess is dead. Crackpots are mourning her and putting up white and pink flower tributes everywhere."

"These people are crazy. Do you think the doctor helped the Princess escape?"

"No. I reviewed the hospital security footage myself. The seven people who arrived to take her knew precisely which ambulance to hit and were perfectly coordinated. They were armed with needles and took out the staff so quickly that no one even had a chance to realize there was a problem. The doctor tried to fight them off. These guys even helped the staff slide gently to the ground as they fell unconscious. It's amazing no one was killed, considering the other attacks. The Princess wasn't even unloaded."

"I have to say that doesn't sound like our usual insurrectionists."

"Can we call them insurrectionists, Grayson? We invaded them."

"As I'm about to spend my entire personal savings on food to get this country through the winter, they'd better start thinking of me as the new King."

Finn reached across the desk and took Grayson's beer and drank from it. "I wonder..." He peered into the mug at the golden liquid.

Grayson's eyebrow went up.

Finn swirled the liquid about. "The people that got me out of the castle were well-coordinated, too."

"The same?"

"Do you suppose this country has another operational group? The insurrectionists, as you call them, are spread out and well-armed, but they don't appear to have a central leader or a master plan." Finn set the beer down.

"Damn effective though. The Demense lords say they can't keep sending more troops."

"If they wanted to kill the royal family before, they could have. They're strong enough."

Grayson shook his head. "I disagree. They hit local targets quite effectively and are causing my peacekeeping troops trouble, but they don't have the transport necessary for a full invasion. The people here have groundcars and those are rare. We brought in a fleet of airships filled with trained, armed men and we pounded the castle with overwhelming force. Scale-wise, the insurrectionists are just raiders."

"Ok. I'll give you that, but the group that whisked me away from the castle was different. That was a precision guerrilla maneuver. Within the first hour, I was moved six times by different people. There was no waiting, no words exchanged. I never heard or saw whatever secret codes they were using. They only said what they needed me to do. No casual chatter. Clothes that fit me were provided; my hair was even dyed."

Grayson hit the table with his fist. "The Princess' hair was cut short and dyed."

"She's with that group of people right now, then. I'm sure of it. A third operating faction. Let's call them... the rivals. We have us, the insurrectionists, and the rivals." Finn stood and started pacing. "The rivals are organized, with the ability to move secretly anywhere inside the country."

"And outside. They got you to Demense." Grayson shifted in his chair. "Why would Noah tell me she's still alive? Is he part of the rivals or isn't he?"

"Maybe he needs your protection? He must want you to find her. Needs you to stop her."

"I really can't waste resources looking for a dead person."

"But who are the rivals? Are they the Princess' personal army? Maybe her plan was to use us to kill the King and Prince so she could take the throne?"

Grayson rolled his head, stretching his neck. "I need you to find out. Our best bet would be to get someone inside the group. You met them."

"They aren't going to let an outsider in. They were solidly organized and unbelievably cautious."

"Start with Noah's surveillance then. Maybe we'll get something there. I doubt we'll get anything from Pieran, but the Princess may try to reacquire her old slave if she's still alive. He shouldn't have been taken into custody in the first place."

"I'm on it." Finn bowed and backed toward the door. "Your Majesty."

Grayson threw a book at him and Finn easily dodged it.

****

Begin Transcript, Session 1

"Noah, do you know why you're here?"

"Yes. The King can't imagine any reason I would be loyal to Milady that isn't a threat."

"By 'milady', you mean the late Princess, Sophie Renault?"

"Sophie, yes, but it would be disrespectful for me to call her by her first name."

"You're aware that she was a war criminal, responsible for killing and hurting countless people?"

"That's what many people think."

"And you don't? Even the King directly witnessed it."

"I know she's done horrible things. She told me about them."

"Yet you're still loyal to her?"

"I trust her. She isn't dead."

"You think she's still alive?"

"Her body wasn't delivered to the King. That was the agreed signal if she was truly dead."

"Who agreed?"

"We did. Milady and I."

"If she's still alive, what if she decides to hurt you? Would you still be loyal to her?"

"Milady no longer has a reason to hurt me."

"So if there's a reason, it's ok to hurt someone?"

"It's never ok. That's the point."

"I'm not following your logic, Noah."

"I volunteered to be here. Anything you guys do to me is my responsibility, not hers. I didn't have to come."

"She didn't threaten you?"

"No."

"Threaten your mother?"

"No."

"Your father?"

"My father died in one of the Prince's dungeons."

"Brother or sister?"

"I'm an only child. I was supposed to go to the Wallace Lords, but I ran away and came back home. I couldn't let Mom stay alone. Milady didn't threaten me. She simply said she needed someone and asked if I would help."

"Were you afraid to say no?"

"Of course not. I was scared to say yes. I did because she needed someone she could rely on. You can ask me this same thing in as many ways as you like, but Milady explained what was at stake, what she needed, and said I would probably be arrested. I volunteered."

"What were you told to do exactly?"

"To be there when she met with the King. To help her walk for as long as I could. And then, if arrested, to try to find Pieran and tell him about recent events. If I had a chance to speak with the King, I was told to ask for Pieran's release again, and to mention the upcoming winter food problem. She told me to endure until the King released me and to speak the truth after she was no longer in custody."

"Endure?"

"Our new King isn't our enemy. Mom's not going to send me back to the Wallace Lords now."

"But the King will arrest Sophie Renault for war crimes if she's still alive. You can't support both him and her. They're on opposite sides. Your logic is still flawed."

"As you said, she hurt people. If I'm allowed, I'll testify on her behalf, but I'll abide by our new King's judgement. It's wrong, but Milady begged me to."

End Transcript, Session 1

Notes:

Noah exhibits no physical behavior that suggests fear or trauma beyond typical anxiety to be expected for his current situation based on his age. The irrational declaration that Sophie Renault is alive despite evidence, however, needs exploration. His insistence on using the title 'milady' for her indicates that he spent significant time with her and that the traumas he endured during that time are deeply buried. The admiration and love in his voice when he says the term is symptomatic of extreme conditioning. It will take time for him to acknowledge what he went through and even longer to recover.

Finn crumpled the paper in his hand. He'd seen the inside of one of those dungeons. He was still fighting off nightmares every evening and he'd just seen, not experienced it. That poor kid hadn't had a chance.

****

Pieran groaned as he climbed from the aircar. His old muscles were stiff and his bones creaked in protest. At least he had new clothes that were clean and of a decent quality.

"Are you sure this is where you want to be dropped off?" the guard/driver asked.

The Larmont Market was busy with foot-traffic, horse-drawn carts, and ground vehicles. It was far enough from Risell to prevent any suspicion that he was headed back there.

"Yes, I have a friend who works here. Thank you for bringing me." Pieran strode off in a random direction. Anything to get away from the guard. The Prince would have taunted him with freedom only to yank it away at the last moment. Pieran knew the new King wouldn't do that, but he couldn't help his ingrained responses.

Once Pieran was sure he was lost in the crowd and couldn't be found again, he slowed and spent a brief moment enjoying the fresh, concrete-free air and sunlight. He didn't even mind the smell of the horses and inadequate sanitation. He went over to one of the booths and asked to borrow a phone. He was given one without question; perhaps his desperation was more apparent than he thought? This place, so far from the castle, also didn't have the same level of caution he was used to.

Pieran dialed one of the pickup numbers. He had to find out what was going on now that Sophie was dead. The sudden, overwhelming loss hit him like a tidal wave. Straightening his shoulders, he focused on what he could do. His country still needed him.

"Kiev's Livestock and Seeds." The chipper voice was almost comical.

"Yes, I'd like to place an order for delivery."

"Of course, Sir. What can I get you today?"

"I would like a bale of hay, 115 pounds of barley seed, and a signed receipt." Pickup for one male, 115 pounds, and a method of communication.

"We have a special today on livestock medical supplies. Would you like any of those?"

"No, thank you. I'm waiting on something else just now at the Larmont Market in Beyers. Is there a chance you can deliver it here by the end of the day?"

"Let me check our schedule, Sir." There was a pause and then, "Yes, we can arrange your delivery in 30 minutes. Perhaps you can meet us with your vehicle at the northern parking lot?"

"Yes. I'll do that." He hung up, thanked the woman who had lent him the phone, got directions, and started the long walk toward the north end of the market. He wasn't used to the exercise and tired easily. His stomach growled and he told himself that he'd be fed soon.

He saw a stand selling different kinds of dried beans and recalled how picky Blair had been about bean selection and he almost wept. The unexpected memory nearly paralyzed him. He stumbled past without a second glance.

The car with the temporary sign on its door for Kiev's Livestock and Seeds pulled through the lot slowly. Pieran flagged it down and got into the back without a word.

Four changes later, he finally spoke to the driver. "Code: starfish alpha eight six."

The driver glanced into his mirror toward the backseat. "Ah. Where to?"

"Central."

"I don't know how to get there."

"Call it in. They'll send someone for me."

The driver pulled over at the next fuel station. "Who should I say you are?"

"Describe me to them. They'll know," Pieran assured the driver. He leaned back tiredly.

The driver returned and got into the vehicle. "I'm to take you to my house, Milord, and give you food and a bed for the night. They'll send a groundcar for you in the morning."

"Thank you."

Dinner in the modest home was odd, without any talking. Pieran almost wished for conversation; he'd gotten used to it in the prison with the other inmates. He also needed real information. Anything Noah had said was now deprecated. The rule regarding unnecessary conversation remained intact, though, for the safety of everyone involved.

Pieran's host gave him new clothes and a wig and he settled in to watch the main media channels. The news stories weren't accurate, but even extrapolating, the truth suggested that their country was imploding, divided into unnecessary combats that killed innocents on both sides. The more Pieran watched, the more urgency he felt. Luckily his pickup arrived shortly after dark to take him directly to Risell. He had a lot to do.

****

In the advanced surveillance mobile compound, Finn sighed in defeat. The bug/tracker was useless. Pieran had switched clothes and the ones with the bug had been dumped at a secondhand shop. They had surveillance around the driver's house and were watching. By midday, they still hadn't seen the pickup. Their advanced audio surveillance also couldn't tell them if the two men were still silent or if Pieran had gone already.

Grayson was going to be annoyed when he got this report. What had they just released from prison? Certainly not some beaten, tortured slave. That pickup was definitely the rivals.

"Sir?"

Finn turned to the young woman. She couldn't be that young, he thought, staring at her rank insignia. "What is it, Lieutenant?"

"We picked the target up on the new cameras in Risell. Facial recognition got him. He switched clothes and had a wig."

"Where in Risell?"

"A clothier, Sir. We had one of our field agents place a bug in the shop almost immediately - sheer luck on that. The bug was supposed to go somewhere else and we simply hijacked it."

Finn glanced up at the ceiling and closed his eyes in a quick, silent prayer. "Do we have the feed?"

"Well, yes and no, Sir. We have the feed, but there's nothing on it. The target disappeared into the back of the shop so whatever they're saying, they're doing it out of range."

"Get one of our advanced audio units in place."

"We're already working on that. We should have something within the hour. Risell is my op location and why I was sent to brief you. To say the town is paranoid is an understatement. Anyone new isn't trusted and everyone watches who comes and goes. We've had some success billeting troops there, but those individuals are tolerated, not included."

"Like an occupied territory in a war zone?"

"Exactly, Sir."

"Let me know if you get anything at all."

"Yessir!" She saluted and left.

Finn grinned and went to shower and shave. Maybe this operation was recoverable, after all?

****

Pieran settled into the chair across from Jo. That was Madame Violet's real name - Jo. He could finally use it. Madame Violet had been her mom and Jo had kept the name so she wouldn't draw attention when she moved back into the area. Jo had insisted that he shower and change clothes before debriefing him. It was a necessary security step, just in case. Did they even need the old security? The smuggling network was still in place, despite a lack of customers and tasks. He was certainly thankful for the available pick-up.

Jo pushed a cup of hot coffee at Pieran. "Noah?" she asked timidly.

"I saw him in the prison and he was fine. Six days ago, guards came and took him away and he wasn't brought back. I'm not sure where he went." Jo paled and Pieran shook his head. He continued, "You don't have to worry. I'm sure he's ok wherever he is. Our new King is a good man. Honestly, I've never felt safer than I did in his prison."

"Sophie was beaten in his prison."

"What?" Pieran set the coffee back down without drinking any of it. "Tell me what happened. Is that why she died?"

"She's not dead."

Pieran bowed his head and put his hand over his heart, letting the relief work through his body.

Jo said, "Noah should have told you. Sophie directed us to give her body back to the King if she died so he'd know for sure. No body. No death."

"I only got word after Noah was gone. He didn't have a chance to tell me that."

"She'll wish she were dead. She's not going to be walking for a long time. Crushed hip and pelvic bone."

"That wasn't Wyatt," Pieran said. That wasn't the Prince's style. He liked to torture his creatures, not permanently damage them. "Noah said the Prince had her for 12 hours?"

"She has Wyatt's signatures. And more. He seemed to rush his normal progression in her case. We tried to make her stand down, but..."

"She wouldn't."

Jo nodded and continued, "Noah took her to meet with the Wallace Lords. They've been warring with our new King. She wasn't physically up to the task."

He wrapped both hands around his coffee cup and took a sip before answering. "I can see how that would happen. They're a contentious group." They'd become that way out of a need to protect their local people from the King and his son. If she was physically wounded and on medications, she probably couldn't argue effectively.

Jo said, "Noah told me they're trying to make her Queen."

"What did she say to that?"

"To call her Milady and to give our support to the new King." Jo reached across the table and put her hand on his. "It's why she wouldn't send anyone to rescue you. We offered. We begged. She refuses to do anything against him."

"She can't. If she crosses that line, she has to take the throne."

"Maybe she should. She was barely holding on when she concocted that idiotic scheme to turn herself over to the King. She said she'd trade herself for you, because you would have the stamina for the Wallace Lords. But he would never trade and she knew that. She made us put children in danger to guard her, promising that the new King wouldn't hurt children."

"He didn't, did he?"

"No, but she made us do that. She said that if he hurt a single child, we should call the Wallace Lords and the rallying cry of justice would finally pull them together and we had her permission to burn the castle to ashes."

"She wanted you to know you can trust our new King, Jo. The children weren't in any danger."

Jo frowned and spat, "She took Noah with her, Pieran, so he could be arrested. To pass along information to you, she said. She put him in danger. My son. In danger."

"If Noah had told her no, Sophie would have found someone else. Be proud of him. He's a brave man."

"But where is he? Where is my son?"

"We'll find him," Pieran promised, and then added, "As soon as I get the Wallace Lords under control."

"Consider this before you meet with them - sometime during our new King's custody, Sophie was beaten, crushed, and left in a cell to die. He failed to protect her from the Prince and he may be responsible for her new wounds."

"What's she say?"

"She hasn't said anything. The doctor has her in an induced coma. Even if she lives, the medical staff thinks she's going to be catatonic. That's if she doesn't have brain damage from cracking her skull on the cobblestone during the arrest."

"She's stronger than that Jo. If she was going to break, she would have long before now."

"Not this time, Pieran. You didn't see her. She may be better off dead and we should seriously consider helping her along that path."

"No."

"Blair isn't here anymore. Anyway, I believe Blair would say, 'What's one more casualty in this war for our victory?' We got rid of the King and Prince, Pieran. We have to let that be good enough."

"No. It's non-negotiable. She lives or dies on her own willpower, not our decision. We have to give her a chance. We owe her that. Get me transportation out to Cymere."

****

Finn read the transcript and felt his stomach drop. The Princess was still alive. The rivals were about to join with the insurrectionists. Grayson needed to mobilize his army and get ready. Finn needed to get to Grayson and warn him and he didn't trust their secure communication lines enough for this. Their computer specialists insisted the country's networks were entirely compromised. They were still rooting out monitoring and tracking software.

Finn's chair fell over backwards as he scrambled, running for the door.

Chapter 6

"Your Majesty, the POWs in Cymere are calling in and asking for transport."

"What?" Grayson tore his attention away from the supply distribution problem. Cymere was currently held by the insurrectionists. He couldn't send troops there without losing them. It was the largest group currently fighting him.

"They're saying they were released. No negotiations. No threats. No messages for you. Nothing. Some old man simply left a key on the floor, barely within reach of our men and then left. They got brave enough to take the key and let themselves out and found the place deserted. No guards, no locals with guns. Just an empty fortification."

"Bombs. They'll bomb when we go in for pickup."

"They have people checking for that. They haven't found anything yet."

"Ok. Have them walk a mile south out of town and we'll pick them up there."

"Yes, Your Majesty."

"Have Finn call me, too. I need to know if he has anything on this."

"He just arrived. The Captain's briefing him."

****

Sophie's eyes fluttered open half-way.

"Doctor, she's awake." The man's voice came from her right.

Sophie turned her head and blinked until the man came into focus. He looked familiar, but she couldn't place him. His white scrubs with light-toned geometric patterns identified him as a medtech.

A woman moved into view, gently pushing the man out of her way. This woman was definitely familiar and also in white medical scrubs, but Sophie couldn't associate a name. Maybe she'd never been told it for security?

The woman leaned close. "Do you know who you are?"

Sophie felt like she was floating. How had she gotten here? She recalled being beaten in the cell and not being able to move. She tried nodding, but the movement hurt.

"I'm going to check your eyes." The woman took a light and held Sophie's left eye open and shined the light in and then the right eye. "Good. You have normal dilation. I want you to try moving your right hand."

Sophie wiggled her fingers, or at least she tried to. The tiny spasm seemed disconnected from any actual command.

"Excellent. Left hand?"

The left hand was easier.

"I want to check your feet but I don't want you to move them. Do you understand?" At Sophie's weak nod, the doctor continued, "You had surgery across your lower abdomen and pelvic region. It went really well, but I don't want you stressing the muscles. I'm going to hold your right foot now. I want you to try to move just your toes. Nothing else. Excellent. The other foot now? Wonderful. You're on heavy painkillers so you're going to feel like you are floating for a while. You're safe here. Only the people with us right now know where you are and you're in a weekend camper in the Gressuf Mountains. Do you know where that is?"

Sophie nodded again. She was so tired. She let her eyes close. They could check her mental acuity after she slept.

The next time she woke, the same man was sitting next to her, reading a book. Sophie tried her voice. It came out dry and scratchy and entirely too slow. "What's going on? What's the King doing? What are the Wallace Lords doing?"

"Ah, my star patient is awake again. The doctor is currently sleeping, but I'll wake her up if you'd like."

"No, just tell me what's going on."

"We're off-grid. Last we heard, Pieran was released and had gone to speak to the Wallace Lords. Everyone thought the King was planning some sort of invasion in the outer regions, but it turned out to be a winter food distribution. Rice, grains, and root vegetables that can last through the winter. No cost. He's buying loyalty."

Sophie couldn't believe how suddenly incredibly free she felt. Pieran would handle things. There wouldn't be any more death. Had Noah finally convinced the King? "Anything on Noah?"

"Who's Noah?"

"A friend."

"I'm sorry, Your Majesty. I don't know anything about him."

"It's just Sophie now. Milady, if you must use a title. We have a King."

"But you're the Queen now."

Sophie sighed and closed her eyes again, too tired to argue. When the doctor came in several hours later, Sophie was awake and opened her eyes.

The doctor leaned over and check her again. "Do you know who you are?"

"Yes. Sophie Renault. I remember everything just fine until I passed out in our King's prison. What happened?"

"As you planned. They discovered you were wounded and transferred you to the hospital. We intercepted the transfer and have been treating you ever since."

"Good. I'm not sure I trust their medical staff not to err on the side of killing me deliberately."

"It was precarious for a while, but you're going to recover and after some PT, you should be able to walk again. Want to tell me what happened in the prison?"

Sophie could remember it too clearly. "No. Besides, you know the results better than me. Tell me what you had to fix this time." When the doctor finished detailing the wounds and damage, Sophie said, "I don't feel any of that. Do you know we're safe? Even if the King arrests me. Even if I die. We're safe."

The doctor snorted. "You don't feel anything because I blocked the nerves and have you on a steady drip of strong painkillers through that IV."

"For which I thank you, Doctor."

"Tomorrow I have to start weaning you off it. You'll have some discomfort, but it shouldn't become unbearable."

"Do you have family, Doctor?"

"We're not allowed to discuss personal details, but yes, I have a family."

"They're safe too."

"I'm looking forward to seeing them."

"How long are we here for?"

"Until you can sit up. Then we'll relocate you to a longterm care facility with some of the other victims so the staff wont be so shocked if they happen to see your wounds. You'll have your own nurses and your own room."

"That sounds like I would stand out. Maybe better to just log me in as another patient and let the facility take over however it normally would. They get deniability protection that way - shouldn't be arrested for harboring a war criminal if I get discovered."

"Respectfully, Your Majesty, you cannot withstand another attack. Your system has too much trauma. It would kill you. You cannot allow yourself to be vulnerable."

"Please call me Sophie, or Milady, if you must use a title."

"Of course, Your Majesty. It's time for you to sleep again." The doctor fiddled with the IV and Sophie drifted off.

****

Grayson shifted on the throne. He would have expected the old King to have a more comfortable chair. Finn kept assuring him that these public audiences were necessary and that the people, even the ones that weren't brave enough to come, respected him more for having them. Maybe the old King had never sat here.

The man who approached through the odd crowd of courtiers was roughly dressed. The clothes were worn, but mended, and were likely the best he owned.

He kneeled on the stone floor, just before the royal carpet began. He kept his head down and didn't look up. He started to speak, but had to clear his throat a few times. He was shaking in terror. "Your Majesty."

"You don't have to kneel, Citizen. What is it you need?"

The man didn't stand, but cleared his throat again.

Grayson waited patiently. These people had survived under those monsters and no matter how uncomfortable their fear made him, he had to give them time to adjust.

The man seemed to be on the verge of crying and perhaps fleeing. "Your Majesty, I would like permission to move my family closer to Gressuf Mountains."

"Ah. Citizens no longer require permission to relocate. Of course you can move your family." Grayson sighed inwardly as another part of his soul tried to shred in sadness. These people were so incredibly damaged.

The man swallowed nervously, still studiously staring at the floor. "Thank you, Your Majesty." Without a glance, he scrambled up and scurried from the room.

Grayson was surprised when the next person to enter was Pieran. Pieran shuffled slightly with a limp, looking old and weak. There were some whispers among the courtiers and now that Grayson knew what to watch for, he could see the subtle shifting of feet as some of them backed up slightly, fractionally tilting their heads respectfully. He tried to remember which ones did it. The courtiers were split among the old King's lackeys, abused toys, and apparently, the Princess' people.

Despite stopping just before stepping onto the royal carpet, Pieran did not kneel and he looked directly at Grayson. "Sire, where is Noah, the boy you arrested with Sophie?"

"Psychiatric hospital in Demense. You can visit him if you like."

"I will. I'll take his mom. She's been worried about him."

Grayson decided that it was time to shock the courtiers even more. "Pieran, I'm sorry for keeping you in prison longer than what was appropriate." This resulted in gasps and widened eyes. He bet they'd never heard one of the royals apologize.

"You had more important things to take care of, Sire. I found the time peaceful, restful, and even somewhat healing. Your prison was the safest place I've ever been." He bowed. "Sire." With amazing dignity in that old man's shuffle, he turned and started to walk away.

Those words hadn't been for Grayson. They'd been for the courtiers, who shifted uncomfortably and whispered. Grayson stood. "Pieran."

Pieran paused and turned. "Sire?"

"Thank you."

Pieran nodded once, almost regally, and left.

Grayson returned to the throne and waited for the next person to become brave enough to enter.

****

"You have visitors," one of the orderlies said, coming up to Noah.

Noah almost dropped his paintbrush. His hand jerked and it left a swathe of unsightly green in his blue lake. "Who?" He put the paintbrush in the water and swished it around. He wanted to jump up. Instead, he carefully closed the lid on the green paint jar. The woman in charge of the art supplies was adamant about taking care of the tools. She would refuse to let someone participate if they damaged something and the art hour was the only true relief he got in this weird limbo where everyone thought he was insane.

The orderly grabbed his arm and gave him a not-so-gentle pull. "Come along, Noah."

"I'm coming." Noah swung his feet around and pushed his feet more securely into his slippers. He followed the orderly. He was taken to one of the private counseling rooms and when he saw them, he shouted, "Mom!" and ran toward her, wrapping her in a hug. The return hug was everything he could possibly need and more.

The orderly growled, "No running, Noah. You know better." Thankfully, the orderly left and waited outside of the room, closing the door.

"Mom, Mom! Are you ok?" He leaned back and surveyed her from head to toe. She seemed ok.

"Did they hurt you?" she asked worriedly.

"No, Mom. I'm fine." Noah turned to Pieran. "Please tell me you're here to get me out of here?"

Pieran shook his head. "No. Why do they think you're crazy?"

"I told our King that she isn't dead." Noah hesitated, afraid of the answer. "Is she?"

"She's recovering. Popular media is still insisting she died."

His mom said, "This room is probably bugged."

Pieran shrugged. "The King has his own sources. It's nothing he doesn't know already. As for the doctors..."

Noah cut him off before Pieran could say something that would result in annoying repercussions. "I only see what's on the news in here. Is it true the Wallace Lords are now supporting our King?"

"They aren't happy about it, but yes. The country is finally healing."

"Honey," his mother said, "You need to do whatever you need to to convince these people you aren't insane."

"Milady instructed me not to lie."

His mom winced. "She could not have meant for you to stay here."

"It's not so bad, Mom. No one hurts me. There's food. I'm learning to paint. Next week, I should have enough points to walk outside in the garden." He wouldn't tell her about the humiliating showers and forced group-therapy sessions that were making him crazy. His therapist routinely lectured him on how his participation would help him recover faster.

"Paint?" his mom repeated.

"It's kind of fun. I'm making a lake landscape at the moment." At her pained and sad expression, Noah wrapped his arm around her shoulders and led her to one of the chairs. "Tell me about Risell, Mom. Are the people adjusting?"

Pieran also sat down, mouthing 'thank you' at Noah behind his mother.

His mom answered, "The King is allowing people to go where they want without requiring permission. Most of the people have moved away. I didn't want to leave in case you came back. The houses are now mainly occupied by the King's army, but aside from some drinking and late night noise, they don't bother us. Some of them even commissioned clothes from me."

"Good," Noah said. "I'm glad you're doing ok. I was worried."

His mom leaned over to Pieran and said, "My son worries about me. He's in here and he worries about me."

Pieran grinned. "Your son is a fine man, Jo."

Noah kept the conversation going by asking his mother about different people and changes in Risell. When the visit was over, Noah went back to his bed and cried into his pillow until they called for lights out and then he tried to sleep. He'd need his mental focus to deal with the next day's therapy sessions.

****

Jo nearly dropped the teapot as she filled it. She should never have gone to visit Noah. Why was this man here? She knew him, that is, she'd seen him the afternoon they'd rescued him from the Prince. Here he was back in the country as the right hand of their new King. She hadn't heard of the new King torturing anyone for information yet, but she knew this man was here to find out where Sophie was. Could Jo last long enough for Pieran to get her moved? Had Pieran already been picked up?

How long it would take him to ignore her son's plight and ask about Sophie? She turned on the burner to heat the water and sat down at the small table. "You said you wanted to ask about Noah, Milord? Are you going to release him?" she said. She kept her voice neutral and reserved.

He shifted uncomfortably on her wooden kitchen chair. "The doctor says he's resisting therapy."

Jo considered her responses. What would it take to get this man to let her son out? The psychiatric hospital staff had been infuriating and after several arguments, they'd suggested she needed therapy herself. Pieran had dragged her out. Jo tried, "It's not resisting to tell the truth, Milord."

He hesitated and then said softly, "The King will protect you both from her if you let him. If you tell him where to send his men, he can rescue people."

How dare he! Did her son not even warrant two direct queries? "Milord, Sophie is not the evil creature you think she is. You're only here because she ordered your rescue from the furnace pit."

"She sent me to the furnace pit," he snarled. "Ordered me to be whipped every hour."

"Consider yourself lucky," Jo snapped. "The Prince was about to order you to his dungeon for training!"

"I don't know how she has you fooled. The King told me what happened. I've seen the scars on his back. Shoot, even Pieran should've told you the truth by now. I know what they do. I've been inside the Brennan's Creek dungeon."

Jo almost retorted that Sophie had been inside it too, but she realized she needed to control her temper. Instead of responding, she stood to check the teapot. She needed to get herself under control. It would be too easy for him to trick her into saying something she'd regret. Her hand was shaking as she tapped the side of the teapot. The water wasn't heating nearly fast enough. She turned the heat up and returned to her chair.

She rested her hands on the table and stared at them. She had age spots and wrinkles and so many years hiding in terror. Hadn't Sophie directed Noah to tell the truth? Maybe it was time? Maybe this man might be able to understand? "Milord, I'm sorry. I meant no offense." She kept her eyes on her hands and the table, deferentially. "May I try to explain?"

"Go ahead," he said angrily. "I want to know what twisted lunacy you people are using to justify protecting her."

Jo inhaled deeply. Thinking carefully, she began, "Suppose you were subject to a psychopath and a sociopath and witness to every vile corruption they forced on others. You'd even experienced some of it, but were mostly protected by your position. Everyone you care about is in danger. What would you do to stop them?"

"Whatever I could," he said tersely.

"Would you risk a chance of failure for a quick finish and possibly let them continue to violate innocents forever or would you plan and work toward a guaranteed victory?"

"Plan, I suppose."

"But you have to survive while applying that plan. You have to somehow secretly acquire a massive, trained army capable of fighting the in-place militia."

"I still wouldn't hurt anyone," he growled. "I wouldn't be part of their demented cruelty."

"Every year, on your birthday, you're given something. Say, a kitten. Cute, adorable, innocent. You're forced to hold it, pet it, cuddle it, and then it's taken from you and sliced open, tortured, and endures agonizing pain for hours, while you're forced to watch."

"I wouldn't allow it."

Jo nodded. "That's a reasonable response. You can object. You can interfere. But it will be worse. The sociopath, whom you have witnessed do this very thing, says, 'Fine. I'll leave the kitten alone. I'll use this child instead.' The kitten still dies of its wounds or from being thrown across the room into a wall, but now a child also dies. Tell me, Milord, do you kill the kitten before it can be tortured, while you are holding it, cuddling it?"

"No."

"How many times would you sit through this before realizing that sparing the kitten that torture is a mercy?"

"No. I still wouldn't. It's vile."

Jo pressed on, "Suppose your gift one year is a new slave. A proud man, used to being free. He's obviously an innocent and has no understanding of the depravities waiting for him. You can't protect him, like you did his friend, but you can make him superficially wounded, drug him, and make him unable to participate."

"No." He shook his head in denial.

"Yes, Milord. You choose to save him, even thinking he may be a perverted spy for the sociopath, because the alternative will kill even more of your soul." Jo hesitated and then said, "Would you like to see the tunnel we brought you through blindfolded? It's below us. Sophie ordered Pieran to get you out, overruling his objections. The Prince was so furious at your disappearance that he had the entire staff of the furnace pit executed. We never told Sophie that."

"It's not possible. I saw the video of her leaving the castle with the Prince. She was happy to go with him."

"Milord, what do you imagine she could have done? He took her directly to Brennan's Creek." On the stove, the teapot squealed. "Who do you think killed the Prince?"

****

The longterm care facility was going to make Sophie insane. Despite her objections, she was given three dedicated nurses and her own room as well as her own doctor. They kept her separated from the other patients and continued to call her 'Your Majesty' despite her objections. Outside of physical therapy, she wasn't allowed to move around. She had to sit or lay wherever they put her, for however long they put her there. She was allowed to watch or read anything she wanted, except news because that 'might upset' her. She had no visitors, because they were maintaining security and keeping her location secret. All of this was for her own safety and wellness, of course. Her staff were extremely polite and very efficient and effective in their medical treatment, but one of them was always present, sitting with her and making sure her needs were met while enforcing their rules.

The room itself was nice, with pretty sunshine-yellow walls and a window overlooking a bird feeder. Once they'd discovered the merits of never turning the lights off, Sophie at least got some sleep. Winter passed and the spring birds returned to the feeder. Her body, at least, seemed to be healing. She still had a lot of pain. Her nurses were strict and stingy with pain medicine, with unapologetic apologies and mutterings about addiction. They took her outside in her wheelchair on nice days and let her sit in the sun for a few minutes before bringing her in with dire warnings about sunburn.

When the leaves started to turn colors for fall again, they finally let her have a visitor. Noah stood in her doorway and Sophie wondered if he was an illusion. She dismissed her staff, promising that Noah would come get them if there were any problems. She listened to them inform Noah that she was not permitted to move from the bed and that, under no circumstances, was he to discuss politics. He agreed to abide by their rules and shooed them out, firmly pulling the door closed. Sophie expected the nurse was standing outside, listening, making sure no unauthorized discussions occurred.

"Are you real, Noah?" she asked quietly.

"Yes, Milady. I would have come sooner, but I was detained." He took the chair the nurse had vacated.

"How are you?" she said, and then immediately mouthed, "Do you have a vehicle?"

He blinked confused. "I'm doing ok now," he answered.

Sophie held up her hands and pretended to be driving. "How's your mom?"

He mouthed, "Oh!" and nodded. "She's doing fine. She and Pieran have moved out to the Gressuf Mountains. They aren't a couple, but are at least there for each other."

Between gestures and more silent words, she managed to convey that she was a prisoner and needed help. Their spoken conversation was stiff and unnatural as they tried to hold two conversations at the same time.

"You know," Sophie said, "I haven't been outside today. I'd very much like you to take me for a walk. I have a wheelchair over in that closet."

The nurse entered at that moment. She was definitely listening at the door. "It's warm enough outside, but you'll need a sweater, Your Majesty."

Noah's eyes widened at the title, but he didn't comment.

"Have you been out to your mom's new place, Noah?" Sophie asked.

"Yeah, it's really beautiful."

"Good, you can describe it to me on our walk. Would that be ok?" she asked the nurse.

"Of course, Your Majesty. You're not a prisoner," the nurse said, somewhat miffed. She retrieved a sweater from the closet and began putting Sophie's arms into it, although Sophie was perfectly capable of doing it herself now. The nurse brought out the wheelchair while Noah helpfully moved out of the way and stood by the door. With gentle efficiency, the nurse transferred Sophie over.

When Noah moved to take the wheelchair's handles, the nurse instructed, "Watch her feet and see that you don't bump her into anything. Stay on the flat area of the grounds. No hills, not even the slight slope up to the end of the driveway. Slow and steady, no bumps. She's not to get out of the chair."

"Bring the umbrella for the sun too, Noah," Sophie added. "That way we can stay out longer."

Noah nodded and after the nurse opened the door, he carefully pushed Sophie down the hallway. The nurse also opened the front door and followed them out.

When it looked like the nurse was going to follow them around the grounds, Sophie said, "Perhaps you can stay here in the shade. You can watch us from the bench? Surely I'm allowed to spend private time with my friend? I promise we wont discuss politics."

The nurse appeared to debate this, but grudgingly agreed and settled herself on the bench and watched them intently as Noah gently pushed Sophie away. Sophie and Noah talked normally, letting their voices carry back, with Sophie asking about the mountains and the house there, and Noah describing things in absurd detail. After a while, the nurse came over and told Noah to hold the umbrella up, which he dutifully did and went back to talking about the small mountain town where his mom and Pieran had settled.

After a while, the nurse stood up from her watchful seat by the building and looked around somewhat desperately. She dodged inside. Noah, immediately turned the wheelchair and dropped the umbrella. "I thought she was never going to go to the bathroom," he whispered, setting off at a jog toward his aircar. "Are you sure this isn't too bumpy?"

"Go go go! Hurry! She'll be back." Sophie held on and wished for pain meds. The bumps were definitely jarring her hips.

"Pieran is going to be really upset with me," Noah muttered.

They got to his aircar and he threw the door open. As carefully as he could in a crazy rush, got her moved into the car. He saw the nurse frantically waving at him in his rearview mirror as they lifted and sped away.

"Oww. Oww," Sophie moaned, holding her right side.

"Should I turn around?" Noah asked with concern.

"If you do, I'll never speak to you again. Oww. I thought their adamant 'no moving' rule was them being over-zealous. I'm probably going to need a doctor - some pain meds at the very least."

"Where are we going, Milady? I wasn't precisely planning on kidnapping you today."

"I have no idea. I don't care. Anywhere except back with them. Don't misunderstand me. Their care was impeccable, but..."

"They didn't listen to you," Noah finished. "'Your Majesty'," he scoffed. "Idiots. What's with the no politics thing?"

"They were afraid it would upset me."

"Will it?" he asked.

"Should it?" Sophie countered.

"No. I don't know how much you know, but as soon as Pieran was released, he went to the Wallace Lords and had them free their prisoners and made them promise to cease their war. The King sent me to a psychiatric facility because I refused to acknowledge you were dead and I only just got released a week ago. The King has been releasing his own prisoners, based on the violence level of their crimes so we should have enough people for this year's harvest. He allocated some of his troops to help with plantings, but they weren't very good at it. They're not farmers."

"At least he's trying? Is Pieran still ruling the network?"

"Yeah. He's got to be super careful. This," he gestured at the vehicle, "Is a rental and I'm in borrowed clothes. I told him that while he may have the fortitude to stay away to keep you safe, I didn't. It took a week of me arguing with him about it to get him to agree."

The car banked slightly and Sophie whimpered.

"Sorry, Milady," Noah said, slowing down.

"No, don't slow down. I fear that they're pursuing us."

"More likely, they'll call Pieran and have him roast me. He gets weekly reports on your progress. Encrypted, of course."

"Was your arrest and psychiatric treatment very awful?"

"Not terrible at all. Your plan worked. I was able to find Pieran and give him news and then when I saw the King, I think I was able to convince him to release Pieran. He may have already been going to, but I did suggest that he was being cruel for keeping an old, tortured man caged."

"Hah! An old, tortured man. That's brilliant."

"Not untrue, though. The King appeared to feel some guilt over it. He seems like a good man, honorable."

"Yeah, we got incredibly lucky."

"We did. Do you know, no one hurt me the entire time I was in custody? Not a single bump or scratch. They even fed me. Oh, hey, wasn't that place you stayed at before a farm?"

"It was."

"Don't farms generally have vets they call for emergencies with the animals?"

Sophie immediately realized his intent. "Yes! There! I'm certain they'll take me in."

****

Pieran sat in the armchair and glared at Sophie. "I arranged excellent medical care for you." The fire crackled in the fireplace. He'd sent Raymond, Marie, and Noah out driving with strict instructions not to return for an hour. "What are you doing here? You risk yourself, Noah, Raymond, and Marie."

"It was too good, Pieran. Might as well have hung a sign on the door saying, 'War criminal inside. Call her Your Majesty as you arrest her.'"

Pieran frowned. Sophie looked so broken, swaddled in the quilt. Her eyes were unfocused, likely from the drugs the vet had given her.

Sophie continued, "I need a lot of care, but cutting me off from everything isn't helping."

"You weren't cut off."

"We can argue that point if you'd like."

Pieran swore. "I'm trying keep you safe, Sophie. That's all."

"You don't need to. Not anymore. You promised me a balcony when this was over anyway. It's over."

"No!" He ran his fingers through his hair, frustrated. "I'm not going to let you jump off a balcony. Just hold on a little while longer. Let some time pass. Let yourself heal. Grow strong. We'll eventually be able to get the King to give you a pardon. I'm sure of it."

"I think you're forgetting what he saw me do. What I ordered done to him."

"I did this to you, Sophie. I manipulated you. I took a young girl and forced her to endure and be our figurehead."

"I was willing enough, Pieran. He needed to be stopped."

Pieran swore again. "You don't understand, Sophie. I arranged for you to be taken into the dungeon that first time. I needed you to be scared enough to join us. I did that to you, Sophie."

"I know that. Blair told me years ago."

"What?" Pieran gasped.

"You also arranged for my father to find out and retrieve me before Wyatt could do any real damage." Sophie shrugged. "So it gave me some nightmares. So what? You also taught me how to survive it and made sure I had the means and ability to escape. I wouldn't be here right now if you hadn't. I used the step counting and the lock picks and the hand-to-hand combat you made sure I knew. I already knew what to expect so I could focus on escaping. You saved me. Indirectly, we could even say you killed him."

"Do you know how much guilt I've been carrying all these years because of that?"

"Didn't Blair mention she told me? I may have started on account of you, but I was dedicated. Every time I stood on that balcony, I chose to continue. I wanted to die, but it was too important not to. We stopped them, Pieran. We. Stopped. Them."

"I've seen your medical report, Sophie."

"You said yourself that any price was worth paying."

"But you don't have to give your life for it. Not now, Sophie."

"Let me stay here. Raymond and Marie are good people. Hire a nurse companion that will actually listen to me. I'll do the PT. I'll keep my head down. Please."

Pieran sighed. "As you command. But I'm taking Noah when I leave. It's too dangerous for him to be here. We'll put you in bed and you're to stay there. I'll send someone to take care of you in the morning."

The fire crackled and Pieran got up and added a log to it.

When he had retaken his seat, Sophie whispered, "I miss Blair."

"Me, too. Me, too." Pieran studied her. It was hard to imagine that after everything they'd experienced, they might both recover. That would only happen if he could keep her from being found. Noah's stunt had been too dangerous. The King had apparently stopped actively searching for her since his friend's conversation with Jo, but enough people were still screaming for Sophie's blood to make it dangerous.

****

Sophie tickled Sunshine's belly and the kitten bit at her fingers and kicked with her hind legs. The tiny claws didn't break Sophie's skin and the loud purring rumble could be felt all the way to her soul. Sophie heard a knock at the door and glanced at the clock. Adele was early. "Come in, Adele!" she called out, nudging Sunshine's jaw so she couldn't latch onto her finger.

The front door opened and the King stood there. "I'm not Adele."

Sophie's heart stopped and she could feel the blood draining from her face. She froze. It was too soon. She wasn't done healing yet. She wasn't ready. Sunshine wriggled in her now still grasp. Sophie inhaled slowly, forcing her outward appearance to emotionless calm. Her old habits took over automatically.

He stepped forward and closed the door behind him.

Lora entered from the kitchen, saying, "Here's the cocoa..." She spotted the King and stopped, glancing between Sophie and him with concern.

Sophie had to protect Lora. Her voice was not as steady or as loud as she would have preferred, but Sophie said, "Lora, take Sunshine and wait outside."

"Of course." Lora brought the two steaming cups over and set them on the side table by Sophie's right arm and reached for Sunshine.

Sophie couldn't move. She tried, but the part of her mind that sent commands refused. Lora had to pull Sophie's fingers from around Sunshine to take the kitten. Thankfully, Lora didn't comment. Sophie's nurse was used to Sophie's rougher moments. Sophie hoped Lora didn't realize she was was paralyzed with terror this time.

Lora walked around the King, giving him a deferential curtsey as she passed, and left. Perhaps she didn't recognize him.

You can survive this, Sophie told herself. She closed her eyes for a split second, almost a blink, and moved her hands to the chair's arms and started pushing.

"Please don't stand up," he said, moving still closer. Another three steps and he'd be within reach.

Sophie managed to get standing, although her hip and pelvic bones screamed. She'd already done her physical therapy earlier. Sophie bent her knees in the best curtsey she could manage, dipped her head, and said, "Sire."

"Please sit down," he said. His voice sounded honeyed-kind. "Please. If I sit, will you sit too?" He glanced around the room and quickly strode over to one of the fireplace chairs and brought it over, setting it across, but a good distance away, from Sophie, facing her. He perched on it.

Sophie's thoughts went wild. Would it be better to sit and endure the agony of being hauled upright or better to stay standing and get dragged away? She decided to let them work for it. Telling her legs to obey, Sophie straightened, found the chair's arms again, and carefully, ever so carefully, lowered herself down. She stayed stiff with a properly straight back and folded her hands in her lap and waited. She was good at waiting. To take any action usually brought on the nightmare faster. The familiar pose helped steady her.

"I'm not here to arrest you," he said, again with the gentle voice. "I'm not here to take you or hurt you. I just want to talk."

Sophie reminded herself that this was not her brother. This man wouldn't likely lie simply to watch her agonize as he twisted a good promise into something demented and evil. Yet, Sophie vividly recalled him calling her a monster last time they spoke. This had been followed with his soldiers arresting her, and beating her already wounded body to a point where her doctor said Sophie should not have lived. Her pelvic bone had been replaced and her hips pinned. The other damage, well, that wasn't his soldiers' fault and it wasn't going to heal any time soon.

His eyes looked sad, but then, her brother's could also seem sad if it suited his agenda. "I wanted to apologize to you. I heard you were able to stand again and I thought you might finally be well enough to see me."

Only seven people knew her current medical condition and her location. The network was compromised, likely by a bug somewhere. Pieran and Noah would be upset, although it was possible their uncensored commentary may help convince their new King that they were supporting him.

Sophie could do this. She could hold a conversation while hiding her thoughts. She'd done it her entire life. She forced her voice to function. "You don't owe me an apology, Sire. It is I who owe you a great debt. What do you need from me?"

"I had the four men who hurt you fired and they are now serving sentences in my prison."

Four? But it had only been three. "Please don't punish them. Their anger was justified." Sophie could hardly blame them for violent retribution when she herself had enjoyed killing Wyatt. It wasn't their fault that they thought Sophie was her brother's equal. Pieran, Blair, and Sophie had hidden their real purpose and attitude extremely well. They had to be good enough at the deception to convince Wyatt, and he was adept at reading and manipulating people. Sophie hated thinking about her brother. She needed to focus.

The King tilted his head to the side slightly and said, "I shall have them released on my return."

Sophie wondered if he was playing with her. She had to believe he was honorable, but her instinct told her not to trust him. He thought Sophie was a monster. "There were only three," she said.

"Only three?" He squinted at her.

Sophie nodded, barely moving. "Only three men." Her voice was still too timid. Her brother would have pounced on that. She'd grown weak as time passed, probably from too many hours holding a purring, sleeping kitten.

"Ah," he sighed, chest deflating and his shoulders dropping. "I think I know which one. I'll have the truth from them."

Sophie waited. She could hear the birds outside. How many men were out there waiting to take her to a cell?

After a moment, he said, "I'm sorry I didn't listen to Noah when he asked for Pieran's release."

Sophie was sorry about that too. Those townships had been painful to get to and they hadn't listened to her either. They'd been too busy shouting about making her Queen to obey her. Sophie replied, "We thought you were one of my brother's spies. If we had known who you were, we would have given you everything. Passcodes, troop locations, codes to the dungeons, the locations of the traps."

"Yes, I finally got the note you sent Noah to deliver to me. The attack was chaotic enough that the lieutenant who'd taken it hadn't remembered. He found it still in his pocket last month."

Sophie's handwriting, hastily scratched during the invasion as Madame Violet was cutting off her hair, had listed the security codes to the dungeons that would have prevented the explosive detonations. "It doesn't matter now," Sophie breathed softly, silently begging forgiveness from the ghosts of those poor, unrescued, tortured souls.

Sophie, forcing herself to bravery, asked, "Is that why you aren't arresting me?"

"The charges have been dropped. There will be an announcement tomorrow morning. No more hiding unless you choose to. I'm listing you as one of the victims so the fanatics will stop screaming for justice, and so you can qualify for the medical and financial assistance we've already granted to the other victims."

Sophie wasn't a victim. Sophie was the victor. She'd won. Pieran, Blair, Jo, and Sophie had won. They'd taken down the Prince before he could ascend the throne. Sophie's father had been cruel and psychotic, but he at least ruled the kingdom. His son had been magnitudes more evil and would have burned the entire country simply to hear the screams.

"Or..." He hesitated and then continued, "I could announced your return to the country as Queen. You could come back to the castle and I could stay and help you until you were able to take over completely, and then I would go home."

"For a moment there, I thought you were going to propose."

The corner of his mouth quirked. "I'm sorry I was so hateful when you offered that as a solution."

"I'm not sorry you turned me down. It would have been a miserable wedding night for both of us." Sophie might have jumped from a balcony if he had tried to touch her. No, she would have.

His fingers rubbed together unconsciously. "You are the rightful Queen by blood. It's your country."

"Are you unhappy being King?" Sophie could weep, if she were capable of such a thing. It really wasn't fair to demand he not only come rescue their country, but that he should be burdened by it as well. And yet, if Sophie had to take over, she wouldn't ever get to rest. She wouldn't ever have the possibility of healing. Hadn't she given enough to this country already? "You're a good King, Sire. When the harvests failed, you brought in relief so the people didn't starve. You listen to complaints fairly and make reasoned decisions. Your new laws are benefiting the majority. You've improved relations with our neighboring countries."

"I'm not unhappy. I'm just not willing to continue if you are going to show up in a couple years with an army, demanding my head, and retake the country. The townships nearly managed to overthrow me once, and that was when they were disorganized. I think we would have fallen within months if you hadn't stopped them."

"Pieran stopped them."

"At your command." He shifted on the chair. "The country is still divided. The commoners are loyal to you. My troops and most around the castle follow me. I think what's left of your father's people are still deciding."

"Sire, I do not now nor will I ever want to rule this country. I want to watch a kitten grow into adulthood. I want to walk in the field of wildflowers out there. Without assistance." Sophie lifted her hand and pointed toward the window and then set it back in its place atop the other. "If you are unhappy or unwilling to continue as King, I will do my duty. The people need to be protected." But please don't make me, she thought. She hurt too much and didn't have the stamina to meet the need. By time Sophie would have it, the country would be entirely different anyway.

He nodded. "I'm not unhappy. Truthfully, if I were to vacate now, my father would kill me." He must have seen her eyes widen or something, because he quickly added, "Figure of speech. He'd be angry. He wouldn't actually kill me. He'd get over it." He exhaled and inhaled again. "But I don't want to be constantly looking over my shoulder worrying about a revolt. I want to make permanent changes and be the true monarch. It's up to you. I'm offering the country to you right now, free of any bloodshed, with any help I can provide to get you situated into the position. Or you permanently abdicate to me, publicly if possible, with me on one side, Pieran in the middle, and you on the other, with Pieran also announcing his support."

Good. He knew the people would listen to Pieran. If it were just Sophie, they'd think the King was threatening her somehow. "I'll tell Pieran your command, Sire. We'll attend at a time and place of your choosing. Simply send word."

He nodded and stood. When Sophie also started to rise, he shook his head. "If you stand, Milady, you will be disobeying a direct order from your King." His gaze seemed to dare her.

Sophie tilted her head deferentially instead and said, "Sire." Was it possible he was telling the truth? This was when her brother would have come in for the kill. Her tiny flame of hope would have been extinguished along with more of her heart.

The King put his chair back into its place and went to the door. Hand on the doorknob, he said, "Will Noah accept a position as one of my advisors?"

"He could be persuaded, Sire."

"Good. I'll send you a messenger at the start of the week."

"Thank you, Sire."

He disappeared through the door.

Lara entered shortly thereafter and came over to Sophie. She said, "Here, Milady. Sunshine was sleeping just a moment ago, so she'll likely fall asleep again quickly." Lara turned Sophie's hands over and set Sunshine into her palms. Sunshine purred a moment, pushed at Sophie's palms with her tiny feet, and fell over into a curled ball of warm fluff.

"Bring my phone," Sophie whispered. She could almost breathe again when Lara came back. Sophie dismissed Lara and dialed Pieran. "The King was just here. Either you or Noah is likely bugged, but leave it in place. I need you both to come. We have the final victory."

Made in the USA
Middletown, DE
16 November 2022

15174153R00077